A King of Shadow

A Shade of Vampire, Book 36

Bella Forrest

Also by Bella Forrest:

A SHADE OF DRAGON:

A Shade of Dragon 1
A Shade of Dragon 2
A Shade of Dragon 3

A SHADE OF KIEV TRILOGY:

A Shade of Kiev 1
A Shade of Kiev 2
A Shade of Kiev 3

BEAUTIFUL MONSTER

DUOLOGY:

Beautiful Monster 1
Beautiful Monster 2

DETECTIVE ERIN BOND

(Adult mystery/thriller)

Bare Girl
Write, Edit, Kill

For an updated list of Bella's books,
please visit www.bellaforrest.net

Join Bella's VIP email list and she'll personally send you an email
reminder as soon as her next book is out! Visit here to sign up:
www.forrestbooks.com

Contents

The "New Generation" Names List

- **Arwen:** (daughter of Corrine and Ibrahim - witch)
- **Benedict:** (son of Rose and Caleb - human)
- **Brock:** (son of Kiev and Mona – half warlock)
- **Grace:** (daughter of Ben and River – half fae and half human)
- **Hazel:** (daughter of Rose and Caleb – human)
- **Heath:** (son of Jeriad and Sylvia – half dragon and half human)
- **Ruby:** (daughter of Claudia and Yuri – human)
- **Victoria:** (daughter of Vivienne and Xavier – human)

PROLOGUE: JULIAN

My head was banging, as if a bunch of monkeys had crawled into my skull and started crashing cymbals together. Slowly I opened my eyes, shutting them again as bright sunlight blinded me. I groaned and sat up.

What happened last night?

Too swiftly, it all came flooding back—Benedict standing over Ruby's body, staring at me with those cold, dead eyes. My body broke out in a shiver that reached my bones.

I shaded my eyes and looked at my surroundings. I didn't recognize anything, but I instantly sensed that I wasn't in Hellswan Kingdom—this place couldn't be more different.

I was in an open-air courtyard, made from white stone with swirling mosaic and semi-precious gems cut into the walls and floor. Huge gold-leaf plant pots were dotted about, with large plants flowing out of them. Branches wound their way along arches and dropped down with heavy, lush fruit.

Ahead of me was a large arch, and beyond that, nothing but sky.

I stood up, clutching at my head as it throbbed. Squinting to avoid the sunlight that was bouncing off the white walls and floor, I staggered toward the arch. Before I could reach it, a woman stepped through and paused at the entrance.

She was beautiful. Unearthly so. She seemed to glow, but it could have been the sunlight. Her hair was long and braided into elaborate twists and plaits, and her clothing seemed to be nothing more than leaves and petals...

Oh.

She was a nymph. The same creatures that Tejus's younger brother had warned me away from in the labyrinth.

I knew then that I should have walked away, but there was something about her...the gentle sway of her body, as if she was dancing while she waited for me…and those enchanting violet eyes. My feet kept walking toward her.

"Greetings, young human," she cooed at me. "You look so tired."

"I am," I found myself murmuring. I *was* tired.

She reached out a hand and brushed my cheek. "We can't have that now, can we?"

"But I must…I must get somewhere," I replied. I couldn't actually remember where I was meant to be—but I was sure it wasn't here.

"Or we could feed the birds together." She smiled, reaching out her arm. A small bird, no bigger than my thumb, fluttered down to land on her finger and chirruped merrily.

"That sounds… nice," I managed, feeling in a daze. "I love birds."

"I bet they love you too," she replied, her huge violet eyes looking into mine. They were so brilliant, like purple diamonds, and I felt like I could have continued staring at them forever.

"Ah, he's awake."

A clipped voice cut through my haze, and I turned to see another woman, a sentry this time, in royal blue robes smiling at me coldly.

The nymph giggled and gave me a peck on the forehead before scurrying off across the courtyard.

"Who are you?" I demanded, taking a step back. "What are you doing here—what have you done to me?"

"What am *I* doing here?" she replied incredulously. "This is my home, boy. It's what *you're* doing here that should concern you."

"What am I doing here?" I asked, a sick feeling churning in the pit of my stomach.

"You have had the misfortune of getting in my way. I have great, glorious plans for Nevertide." She clutched her hands together in glee. "A long-awaited day of glory, marching toward us…and I can't have an inconsequential human ruining it all." Her eyes gleamed with the mania of a zealot.

"You know," she continued as I gulped down the bile rising in my throat, "I've never had a human of my own… I do hope you enjoy your stay, dear Julian. It's going to be a very long one."

Hazel

I stared morosely around the deserted room. Its lavish decorations were faded, the gray stones as bleak here as they were in the rest of the castle. Ruby, Ash and I had stumbled upon this room in our search for Julian. We had already checked the areas of the castle that we knew: the servants' quarters and the human quarters, along with the old rooms of Tejus's brothers—Jenus and Danto. Now, with Ash's help, we were trying to navigate the abandoned rooms and hallways that had fallen into disrepair, neglected for many years. Jenney and Benedict were also off searching, but they had started in the west wing of the castle, searching around the bull-horse stables and the crop storage rooms.

I was trying to keep my mind on the task at hand, but as we searched for Julian, I felt as lost as he was.

The intense kiss I'd shared with Tejus, and the emotional turmoil that went with it, had happened only moments ago—but when we'd been interrupted by Ruby, I'd seen the defensive, cold walls that Tejus had built around himself swiftly go back up. I was already half-wondering if I'd imagined the entire thing, and were it not for the tingling sensations that I still felt where he'd touched me, I would have questioned my sanity. The tender words, his questioning gaze—the small hint of him wanting something more from me, wanting something more from *us*—was so unexpected and out of character. I replayed the moment again and again in my head, holding the memory close to me so that it wouldn't vanish—but the more I remembered, the more his actions resembled a goodbye...and a warning? To stay away?

I didn't know where that left me. I had spent so long trying to block out any feelings toward Tejus—anything that I thought would distract us from the perilous trials and the end goal of getting the Nevertide borders lifted— that I didn't fully understand what I felt toward him. He had been my kidnapper, and then my (almost) friend, and now… now I didn't know. The only thing I had absolute clarity on was the fact that there was a huge lump in my throat, and no matter how much I distracted myself with the search for Julian, it would not go away.

"I'm going to try to use True Sight," Ash announced. "It will be easier from here—we're nearer the center of the castle."

He sat on the floor, and Ruby crouched down beside him.

"Are you sure?" she asked, her arm resting against his.

"Absolutely," he replied. "I'm just going to need…"

"Take whatever you need," Ruby interjected. "It's okay."

I watched their exchange, noting that the closeness Ruby and Ash had been developing throughout the trials seemed almost tangible now. As we'd searched the castle they'd never strayed far from one another, and sometimes it had felt like they were sharing unspoken conversations in their own private bubble. I felt slightly awkward, as if I was intruding, but I was also glad for Ruby. Even as fraught as she was, as we all were, about Julian, she seemed to gain strength from Ash, as if the role of the syphoning sentry had been reversed, and it was Ruby, not Ash, who grew stronger and brighter.

I stood by the window as Ash syphoned off Ruby, their hands held and Ash staring off into the distance—looking through and beyond the walls of the chamber, into the locked rooms and narrow hallways of the castle.

"Nothing," Ash murmured after a while. "I can't see far enough."

Ruby's shoulders slumped in disappointment. "I can't help but think he's left on purpose... What if he's out there now, looking for the borders again?" she said, wrapping her arms around herself as she shuddered at the thought.

"Don't go there—he wouldn't do that," I replied hastily. "I know he was upset that we didn't try harder to lower them ourselves, but he's also too sensible to go on a suicide mission. We'll find him."

The idea of Julian purposely putting himself in danger chilled me to the bone. But I also strongly believed that it wasn't the case—we were children of The Shade, and as familiar as we were with the supernatural, and taught to be independent and resourceful, we also knew that it was selfish and foolhardy to take such risks with our own lives.

"Do you think you could see further—maybe to the grounds—if you syphoned off two people?" Ruby asked suddenly.

Ash shrugged. "I've never tried it… I'm not even sure if I *can*."

"But it's worth a try, right?" Ruby insisted.

"Yes." Ash nodded slowly. "If you're willing, Hazel?"

Both of them turned to look at me. I nodded immediately—if it would help us locate Julian, I was willing to do whatever it took. But as I sat on the opposite side of Ash, readying my mind for the syphoning, I couldn't help but feel nervous. The mind-melding between Tejus and me had become such a personal act that it felt strange to be allowing another sentry to do it— almost as if I was somehow being disloyal to Tejus. It was such an irrational thought that I dismissed it immediately, but it lingered at the back of my mind, joining the other bizarre and conflicting emotions I felt toward the new King of Hellswan.

I felt Ash's mind reaching out to mine—the cold, aching sensation of invisible wisps touching at my temples, as if fingers were slowly pushing into my brain. Ash's hold on me wasn't quite as strong as Tejus's or Jenus's had been in the past, but I could feel my energy slowly being syphoned off. I realized that I hadn't eaten in a while, and it was likely that both Ruby and I weren't at our best, making it harder for Ash to take what limited supplies we had.

Opening my mind up as best I could, trying to push my mental reserves toward Ash, I could almost feel the connection between him and Ruby growing. It was a strange sensation, sort of like watching two bright suns meld together while I stood on the outside, my own glow dim and dying compared to theirs. I could sense our shared determination to find Julian, the one thing that we all had in common, but it was almost overshadowed by the mix of emotions fluctuating between Ash and Ruby—small sparks of frustration and wanting, of unspoken words between the two of them. I tried to block it out, focusing only on Julian and allowing Ash access to my energy, but the feeling that I was intruding on something private intensified.

The door to the room swung open with a bang, and abruptly the connection was broken. I turned sharply to see who it was, and my eyes met Tejus's as he glowered from the doorway.

"What's going on in here?" he asked, his face contorted with barely controlled anger. I jumped up, suddenly wanting to get some distance between Ash and me, as if I'd been caught doing something wrong. I wavered slightly as I stood up, my head dizzy and my legs weak from lack of energy.

"We're trying to find Julian," I replied, rubbing my temples.

Ash turned and glared at Tejus. "I was using True Sight, it was a better way of seeing the castle. The others are off looking—*we're* all trying to do something helpful."

Tejus looked impassively at Ash, as if he hadn't heard a word that he'd said—or had completely ignored all that he'd said.

"Hazel?" Tejus turned to me.

"It's true. We thought if we all mind-melded it would make Ash's True Sight stronger," I replied, maddened by his attitude. If he wasn't going to help, what choice did we have? And really, what was the big deal about me mind-melding with Ash in the first place? I sighed in irritation.

"You're obviously too weak," he retorted, looking me up and down. I was still wearing the lavish gown from earlier, and I was starting to feel ridiculous in such a get-up. I noticed that Tejus had discarded the ceremonial robes he'd been wearing for the coronation, and was wearing his usual uniform of loose black trousers and black shirt. His hair hung loosely down his back, its darkness shading his features, making his eyes seem almost black and the freshly-shaved hollows beneath his cheekbones more pronounced. My gaze was drawn to the stark lines of his lips, drawn in contempt. Looking at him now, I couldn't see even a glimpse of evidence that hinted of our earlier intimacy—and it was only my memories of the taut planes of muscle that lay beneath the black shirt, the coarse hands at my face, and the recollection of how soft and pliant his lips could be, that made me stand, frozen in his line of sight, blushing furiously and feeling unaccountably ashamed.

"When did you last eat?" he emphasized shortly, raising his eyebrow.

Great—we're back to protective Tejus, treating me like a child.

"I'm not entirely sure," I replied dishonestly—I knew it had been yesterday that I'd last had a proper meal.

Tejus stared at me coldly. "I have a meeting with the ministers to discuss lowering the borders. You should attend—if there is time, I can discuss the missing boy...see if we have spare guards. There will also be food."

"His name's Julian," I reminded him, trying to match his detached tone with my own, "and yes, I want to come."

Right now I would give anything to end the uncomfortable atmosphere in the room. Sitting with a bunch of minister sentries for a few hours seemed like a small price to pay. Plus, I was eager to hear the verdict on the borders and how soon we could get them down, along with any extra help we could get finding Julian. One wasn't going to be much use without the other though— there was no way any of us would leave Nevertide without our friend. Julian should be the priority.

"Are you going to be okay?" I asked Ash and Ruby.

Ruby nodded. "We'll be fine—we'll go and join up with Benedict and Jenney. I don't think Julian's anywhere in the castle."

"I don't think so either," I agreed dejectedly. It was starting to look like Julian had gone off in search of the borders himself. Which meant that he would be at the mercy not only of creatures in the Hellswan kingdom, but of the unknown inhabitants of the six other Nevertide provinces.

"Hazel—come," Tejus commanded from the doorway.

You're really pushing your luck, Mister.

My first instinct was to shoot him the finger, but I got a hold of myself and smiled as sweetly as I could, my eyes flashing in a warning. I would *not* be spoken to like a dog—or a child.

I rolled my eyes at Ruby as I departed. For the first time

since we'd arrived at Nevertide, I couldn't help but feel like I'd really drawn the short straw when it came to being paired with our champions.

Benedict

I scrunched up my nose in revulsion. Jenney and I had pushed open a wooden door in the storage quarters and been hit with the strong odor of something similar to vinegar—but much, much worse.

"Pickles," Jenney noted in disgust, prying open a cork top on one of the clay jars.

"Well, he wouldn't be in here," I replied, covering my mouth with my sleeve. We'd been searching for Julian for a couple of hours now, and I was running out of hope. It didn't make sense to me that Julian would be in the castle—with the absence of Jenus the idea of kidnapping was kind of ruled out, which meant that he'd either gone off in search of the Nevertide borders by himself, or…

Don't.

My gut clenched in agitation.

I couldn't forget the picture of Yelena on the ground in front of me, my arms raised up over her—doing *something*. Something that was unspeakably wrong, that gave me a vague queasy, sick feeling. What if I'd done something to Julian while I was sleepwalking? I had so many blackouts, time going missing completely. I'd woken up in odd places around the castle, and then in the weird Viking graveyard where Queen Trina had thankfully rescued me and taken me back.

"Let's get out of here." Jenney started to back away toward the door and, gratefully, I followed her out.

"What's with the food here anyway?" I asked trying to ignore my morbid thoughts. "Why is it so gross?"

Jenney pursed her lips. "Oh, thanks!" she replied tartly.

Oops.

Belatedly I remembered that she worked in the kitchens. She hit me playfully on the shoulder. "Idiot."

"Sorry," I replied meekly.

"Sentries aren't too fussy about food—especially not the ministers and higher-ranking officials. They get most of their energy from minds – each other's, before we discovered humans—not food." She shrugged. "Why would they care about it?" Jenney looked up and down the hallway. "We've checked all these rooms. I think we should go and look around the emperor's room—at least Julian knows that area better."

I nodded, but kept quiet about the flaw in our logic: why would Julian be so close to us—the emperor's rooms weren't far from our living quarters—and not say anything?

"Let's go," I mumbled, happy to at least get out of the dank storage rooms. Other than the vinegar room, everything around here smelt musty and damp, reminding me of the cellar that Jenus had locked us in after we'd been set free by Tejus.

Jenney led me up some stone steps to the main area of the castle, decorated with the familiar tapestries, skeleton vulture heads and aged red carpet. I trudged wearily after her, feeling the effects of my lack of sleep over the last few weeks on top of tonight, but refusing to even think about what I'd been doing instead.

"Do you think Julian would have gone off on his own—tried to get out of Hellswan?" Jenney asked as we walked along a silent corridor.

"No," I replied instantly. It wasn't completely true. I'd

been wondering the same thing, but I knew Julian, and though Nevertide was driving us a little bit crazy, I didn't want to think that he'd done something so...*reckless*.

"He wouldn't," I continued, more to reassure myself than Jenney, "he wouldn't leave us, not even to get help. He knows how dangerous it is out there."

"So did you," Jenney pointed out, "and you still went out with all the kids on one of your Hell Raver missions."

"Hell Raker," I corrected automatically. "We didn't know about the beasts then—or whatever those creatures were." I shuddered. I could still recall their howls perfectly. It wasn't something I ever wanted to hear again.

I groaned inwardly.

Yelena was coming toward us from the far end of the hallway, her pale face glowing in the light of the torches. She waved at us uncertainly.

"What are you doing up?" I asked. Judging by the sliver of light I'd seen far off in the distance at the last window we'd passed, it was nearing dawn. She hadn't been invited to the coronation, so she should have been sleeping under guard in the human quarters.

"I heard Julian was missing," she replied breathlessly. "I've come to help you guys look!"

Great.

"I think we've got everything covered. You should really just go back to bed."

"Benedict," Jenney warned. "Let Yelena help—the more eyes the better."

"Whatever," I replied. Privately I thought we'd do a lot better without her badgering us.

Yelena crossed her arms, her bright blue eyes assessing me with irritation. "I don't know why you have to be so mean. I'm offering to help look for *your* friend."

"I'm not being *mean*." I mimicked her petulant tone. "I just don't want anything slowing us down—like you're doing now."

"You're both slowing us down," Jenney interrupted. "Just behave."

I glared at Yelena. She was already causing trouble. I huffed and walked on, following Jenney.

As we neared the emperor's chamber, the hallways started to look more familiar. Jenney turned a corner a few yards after the doorway to the emperor's room, and I came to a halt. She was walking down the dead-end corridor, the one with the small closet door which led to the glowing stones. No *way* was I going down there. I took a step backward.

"What's up?" Jenney asked, noticing my reluctance.

"Nothing." I gulped. "This is just a dead end—let's go."

"Ah-ha!" she replied. "That's where you're wrong…"

She walked over to the closet and swung the wooden door open. I stared, transfixed, into the gaping blackness of the small passageway.

"This is a hidden passage. I discovered it years ago. One of the kitchen boys told me that it's rumored to lead to the different kingdoms!" she continued excitedly.

"Have you ever been down it?" Yelena asked, practically sticking her head in the passageway to get a better look.

"I've tried, but I've never gotten that far. It seems to go on forever, so I've always just given up. I think it gets smaller too—but if Julian discovered it, maybe he tried to get out this way…maybe he got stuck?" Jenney speculated.

I was having difficulty breathing, and Jenney's words were fading in and out of my consciousness. The blackness of the passage seemed to loom ahead of me, growing bigger and bigger the more I stared into its depths.

"I think we're wasting our time—he wouldn't go down there." I tried to make my words sound as convincing as possible, but my throat felt dry and croaky, and both girls were ignoring me, still peering down into the darkness.

"Benedict, don't be silly. It's actually quite likely. This place isn't far from our quarters. If Julian had seen this, he would have gone down it for sure," Yelena corrected me.

"He wouldn't because we've already been down there—and there's nothing!" I burst out.

"What? When?" Jenney asked. "Why didn't you say so?"

"Because there's nothing *down* there," I replied defensively, avoiding her inquisitive stare. "Why would Julian go down there again if he already knew that?"

"I still think we should look," Yelena replied stubbornly.

No, don't!

"So do I," agreed Jenney. "Are you going to come?"

They both looked at me, and I shook my head.

"There's no point," I replied, trying to sound dismissive, but I could hear the slight tremor in my voice. Jenney looked at me warily, but didn't say anything.

"Suit yourself." Yelena shrugged, bending down to enter the passage.

I wanted to shout out—to stop them. But my voice was stuck in my throat, and what would I say anyway? Queen Trina had told me to keep the stones a secret, to let them guide me. They were supposed to be a *good* thing, but they didn't feel that way. I hoped that the borders I'd felt down there were still in place, and that the girls wouldn't be able to find any more than Julian had when we'd been down there the first time—just miles and miles of empty passageway.

Jenney disappeared through the entrance, and I collapsed against the opposite wall. Sweat beaded at my temples, but my body felt cold all over. There was something *dark* looming in that place. I just didn't know what it was. And I didn't want to know.

Why don't you join them, Benedict?

The whisper came floating from the passageway toward me. The voice was silky soft, almost as if it was caressing the air around me—persuading, trying to draw me in.

"I don't *want* to," I whispered back to the empty hallway, shuffling back against the wall so my knees were up against my chest.

But the stones...they're so powerful.

The whisper came again, its tone knowing and mocking—creeping inside my skull, urging me to rise from my cowering position on the floor. I clutched my knees more tightly toward me, thumping the side of my head with my fist.

Go away! I thought in desperation.

Why do you defy me, Benedict?

I moaned softly. I thought if I heard anymore I would start to lose my mind. My breath was coming in short gasps, and my vision had started to go blurry. I was having a panic attack. I crawled onto all fours, breathing deeply, trying to calm myself and shut off the voice.

"What are you *doing*?" Yelena exclaimed, reappearing at the doorway to the passage.

"Um…I was exercising," I blustered as relief coursed through me. My heartbeat started to slow down, and I rose from my ridiculous position on the floor. "Did you not find anything?" I asked.

"No." She sighed, moving past the entrance so Jenney could also get out. "We had to turn back—there's nothing for miles and miles."

Jenney nodded. "Though I could have sworn I felt something like a barrier there—like there was something blocking our path. Did you get that?" she asked me.

"Yeah, maybe," I replied. "The ministers might have put it there to stop people from getting into the castle without them knowing."

"Good point. Then that means the stories might be true. I bet it *does* lead to the other kingdoms, maybe even out of Nevertide," Jenney speculated.

I couldn't share her enthusiasm. Whatever was down there didn't want me getting out of Nevertide, I knew that much. It just wanted me to take power from the stones—

but why I didn't know, and I wasn't entirely sure I wanted to find out. The one that Hazel had given me—green and glowing with a seemingly never-ending source of energy—weighed heavily in my pocket. I kept it on me for safekeeping, but I avoided touching it as much as possible, hoping that if I didn't 'activate' it, then the whispering voices wouldn't know that I had it until the day I could finally be rid of it for good.

"Shall we find the others?" Jenney asked, sounding a bit fed up.

"Yeah, and I think I need a nap."

Yelena scoffed. "You're such a wimp, Benedict."

If she had been a boy, I would have thumped her.

HAZEL

I sat next to Tejus in a large, high-ceilinged chamber that I'd never been in before. I counted nineteen ministers all seated around us, whispering and muttering as they always did, waiting for Tejus to begin the meeting.

The interior was lavish, with high windows that let in the early-morning light, framed by long, cascading curtains that reached to the stone floor. Rather than the tapestries that I was used to seeing, seven large oil paintings hung about the room, each depicting stern men, all looking strangely similar to Tejus. The one that hung at the far end of the room, behind the ornate throne at the top of the table, was a large picture of the dead emperor,

Tejus's father. He looked as cold and forbidding as I remembered him - like Tejus in so many ways. I recalled the conversation we'd had at the beginning of the evening—how I'd tried to tell Tejus that he had a choice, that he didn't have to follow in his father's footsteps. Had I been wrong? Perhaps it was the only life that Tejus knew, the only one he wanted to pursue, or was capable of living.

I looked at him now, his profile as stark and unforgiving as his father's. As soon as we'd entered the room he'd ordered a servant to fetch me a plate of bread and cheese, but since then he hadn't so much as looked in my direction.

He looked up suddenly, turning toward the door as another man entered. This man looked vaguely familiar to me—I thought I'd seen him in the hallways of the castle a few times, and on the night Tejus had been summoned to the sick emperor. Unlike the rest of the ministers, this man wore maroon-red robes, with a vicious-looking sword in a scabbard at his waist. I guessed he was roughly the same age as Tejus, with similarly distinguished features—a classic Roman nose and the austere jawline—but this man's eyes seemed brighter, and the corners of his mouth betrayed laughter lines that Tejus lacked.

"Commander Varga." Tejus rose and nodded as the

man approached us.

"Your Highness," he replied, bowing low. I saw a small twitch of amusement flicker through Tejus's face, but it vanished in an instant.

"This is Hazel Achilles." Tejus gestured to me and I smiled faintly as I met the commander's gaze, drawing back my chair to stand.

"This is Commander Varga," Tejus informed me. "If I can permit any spare guards we have to look for your missing friend, they will be under Commander Varga's charge."

"Thank you." I nodded at the man, not really knowing what else to say. He was looking at me with curiosity, and I wondered why I was arousing such interest. Perhaps there hadn't been a great deal of humans permitted into this chamber—it was clearly a room allocated for kingdom administration, so perhaps my presence was odd in itself.

"Don't thank me yet," he replied. "My men may still be needed elsewhere." I must have looked downcast, because he smiled at me, his entire face transformed. "Many go missing in Nevertide, don't worry. He shouldn't be too hard to find."

He turned on his heel, bowing once again to Tejus before taking a seat at the table. I wondered if the two of them were friends. It was the first time that Tejus had ever bothered to introduce me to someone in Hellswan, and they certainly seemed at ease with one another—well, as much as I'd ever seen two sentries at ease with one another. The formalities among the ministers and royalty were completely bizarre to me. I'd never experienced such a stuffy, uptight set of people in my life.

What about last night?

The thought came unbidden into my head. I looked intently down at the table, not wanting Tejus to catch my furious blush. Last night…that had been different. Tejus had been different. It was difficult now to compare the cold man who stood next to me with the Tejus who'd held me in his arms, taking my breath from me with every kiss and touch.

"Sit down," Tejus addressed me, interrupting my erratic thoughts. "We need to begin."

A silence settled over the room, the conversations between the ministers petering out as they all turned to Tejus. I wondered why he wasn't sitting on the throne, but perhaps it was reserved for the emperor only—evidence of more stuffy customs.

"Ministers, thank you for your time." Tejus leaned back in his chair, his voice low and unhurried. I couldn't detect even a flicker of nervousness in his countenance, though this must have been the first time he would be addressing them as King of Hellswan. "I've called you here to discuss the borders. Now that the trials are over, and relative normalcy has returned to Nevertide, I command that they all be reopened so that we may dispose of our human charges."

Dispose of our human charges?

Wow.

If I needed any further confirmation that the kiss we'd shared had been nothing more than a goodbye, then his statement to the ministers was absolute proof. I felt like someone had punched me in the stomach, and I could do nothing but stare up at him, taken aback by his audacity.

"Is that wise, your highness?" One of the ministers spoke up in a shrill voice. "We have no emperor yet. We have successfully opened the Hellswan borders, but I do believe that if we open the outer borders we leave ourselves susceptible to threat!"

Tejus sighed in a bored manner before addressing the minister. "Qentos, there hasn't been an outside threat to Nevertide in over a century. There is no risk."

"But—but without the kingdoms aligned under one emperor..." the minister stuttered.

"Enough. This is mad speculation. The humans need to leave—they are many in number, and wasting my resources. Already one is missing," Tejus replied curtly.

I didn't want to hear more. I was desperate to leave the room, to cry away my stupid crush in private, but I had to hear the resolution to the borders – the fact that the Hellswan borders were open was news to me, and it meant that Julian could have gone further than we first suspected if there was nothing stopping him from leaving the kingdom. More than ever, I needed to know if the *king* would allow us guards to assist in the search for Julian.

"Your highness." Another minister spoke up, his eyes sweeping over me. "Let us discuss this matter in private. There is more that concerns us—a great deal more. But it is not for the ears of your"—he waved his hand in my direction—"*human*."

Tejus eyed him, cold dislike seeping across his face.

"Watch your tongue," he replied, each word like a shard of glass hurtling toward the minister. He turned his attention to the rest of the table. "We will discuss this in private, then. But I assure you, before the sun sets tomorrow, I will have your assistance with the lifting of the borders, whether you will it or not."

The ministers all lowered their heads, avoiding his glare.

"The subject of the boy." Tejus broke the silence with a tone that gave no indication of the threat that he'd just made against his council. "I wish to have him located as swiftly as possible. I don't wish more effort to be expended on this than is necessary. Commander Varga, can we spare men?" Tejus turned to the commander.

"We can. Five will be enough," Commander Varga replied in the same brisk tone.

"Your highness—" The first minister wavered.

"What *now*, Qentos?" Tejus interjected in exasperation.

"Should we be expending our men to help with such a…trifle of a matter?"

The minister quailed under Tejus's answering glare.

"These particular humans assisted me in the trials. It is my responsibility—and surely," Tejus continued with a smirk, "you too are grateful, Qentos, that it is I who succeeded in the trials, are you not? Don't you wish to repay the favor?"

"Of course, your highness," said the minister, color rising in his cheeks.

"I thought so," Tejus replied. "Then the matter is settled. Five guards under the command of Varga will seek out the wayfaring human."

I heaved a sigh of relief.

The ministers started to draw back their chairs from the table. There was no muttering now, only the sound of grating wood against stone, and their rapid footsteps as they all hurried from the room.

Commander Varga approached the table.

"Your Highness, I will dispatch the men in an hour." He bowed slightly and then turned to me. "Do you have any indication of where he might have gone?"

"I suppose...we didn't want it to be true, but probably to find the borders. He wanted to get out—but ... but none of us would take him seriously." I stumbled, feeling ashamed that it had come to this. "We were waiting for Tejus or Ash to ask the ministers to lift them..." I stared around the empty room.

What a waste of time that had been.

"You were right to wait. No human can lift them," Commander Varga stated, but not unkindly. "We will find him, Hazel Achilles."

"Thank you," I murmured. I was so grateful for his help, but I couldn't help feeling that we'd abandoned our friend. The last time I'd seen Julian he'd told me that he'd informed Ruby about the stone—and I'd been so annoyed with him, annoyed that he'd exposed my secret. More worried about Tejus being disqualified than Julian's feelings, or even Ruby's feelings.

What had I done?

Commander Varga nodded, and then, after placing a hand briefly on Tejus's shoulder, he left the room. I looked over at Tejus. He was still seated in his chair, looking out to the morning light that was coming through the windows, deep in thought—his brow creased in concentration.

"What's going on, Tejus?" I demanded.

We had gotten so far—so close to getting the borders open, the whole reason that I'd agreed to assist him in the trials—and I couldn't quite believe that we were being held up by a bunch of whispering sentries, who to me all seemed pretty useless in the grand scheme of things.

He ran his knuckles beneath his jaw, and then with a sigh he turned to me.

"I don't know. I don't truly understand their reluctance. To wait until we appoint a new emperor is madness—who knows how long those trials will take…but then the matter of my father's death is still unresolved. I wonder if that is the true motive behind their opposition to my request."

"But that's ridiculous!" I retorted. "Can't we at least lower them just so we can leave—and then put them back up again?"

Tejus smiled bleakly. "It doesn't quite work like that. It takes a tremendous amount of power to uphold such a large boundary—lowering it for even a moment would require a prodigious effort from the ministers. I can't do it without them."

I groaned in frustration. "But they're the ones who put it up in the first place, right? They got the Hellswan borders open – why not the outer ones?"

"I thought so," Tejus replied softly, staring back off into the distance again, the furrow returning to his brow.

"What do you mean, you *thought* so? Who else would have done it?"

A flash of irritation crossed his face, and he glared at me.

"Hazel, I find this as frustrating as you do. I too want the borders opened. But I have to question everything at this stage…there is something that I'm missing here."

That silenced me. What had he said earlier? That the humans were *wasting his resources*. His rejection and dismissal of me hurt more than I'd ever thought words could. Growing up in The Shade I'd understood the dangers of the supernatural—fangs, spells, claws, those were dangers that I was always half-ready for. I'd read countless romances, and I understood the language of heartbreak, but I'd always dismissed it as the bump in the road before people found their happy ending. I just wasn't prepared for it to hurt so…*physically*.

Have I gone and fallen in love with him?

Is that what this pain is?

"Because you want me gone?" I dared to ask—testing my theory, morbidly wondering how much he *could* hurt me.

A long silence ensued, and Tejus wouldn't meet my questioning gaze.

"It's safer for you," he managed eventually.

"Is that the only reason?"

He looked slowly up at me, eyes black, his mouth cut in an uncompromising line, and a faint color burning at his cheekbones.

"Yes."

Liar.

I left him sitting in the council room, moving through the doorway as fast as I could without betraying my desperation to get a million miles' distance between us. When I reached the hallway, I ran.

Ruby

After our fruitless search for Julian, we'd all taken ourselves back to the living quarters. The kids taken in from the trials were all still more subdued than I was comfortable with—I felt that they should have recovered from the mind syphoning by now, but their mental barriers probably weren't as strong as ours.

To get some privacy, Ash, Benedict, Jenney, Yelena and I had all locked ourselves in my room, the largest in our living quarters. As glad as I was that we were all together, I couldn't help but wish Ash and I could get some time on our own. Every so often I could feel his eyes traveling over to me, or he would place a reassuring hand near mine, and

I guessed that he was feeling the same way too. But we hadn't had a chance to speak about what had happened between us after the trials. With all the celebrations and then Julian vanishing, I'd not had a moment to process how I felt about Ash, or really, about *us*.

It felt strange to be having romantic feelings toward a sentry. The supernatural wasn't anything new to me, but before Nevertide I'd never come across anything like the sentries, and there was still so much I felt I didn't know about them as a species—or Ash himself. For the most part, Ash always seemed so *human* to me, but then he would do something, like show me his True Sight abilities, or reference strange food, strange customs, and I would feel separate from him, knowing that our worlds were miles apart.

"What do we do now?" Jenney addressed the room.

I was brought back into the present with a jolt. My focus needed to be on Julian, not my feelings for Ash.

Pull yourself together.

"I think we need to start widening our search, going outside the castle for starters," I replied. "Maybe he hasn't gotten far, especially if he was traveling at night."

Ash looked out of the window. "I don't know…sunset will be in an hour or so, I don't think it's sensible for us to go out at night either."

I followed his gaze. He was right. I could see the darkening sky and the sun slowly turning redder as it began its descent.

"Have we been looking that long?" I asked, confused.

"The days are getting shorter. We're in the ninth moon now. Colder too—another reason I'd say that we should wait until morning to look for Julian again."

I had no idea what Ash meant. Was it that the seasons were changing here already? I looked out at the trees, and I could see the dark greens of their leaves were already starting to yellow and age. Wow. It had seemed like the beginning of summer when we'd arrived.

Did time warp in Nevertide?

I guessed we'd only find out once we left.

"So we wait, then?" Jenney replied resignedly.

"I guess we do." I didn't like the idea any more than she did, but I didn't feel like we had a choice. Maybe if it was just Ash and me on our own, I'd be more willing to venture out—but there was no way I was taking Benedict out of the castle after dark.

"Okay," Jenney replied with a sigh. "Come on, Yelena, let's get some rest."

I looked over at the young girl in the corner. Her eyelids

had already started to droop as we'd been talking. She was leaning, unaware, toward Benedict, who was eyeing her half-asleep form with his arms tightly folded.

"You too, Benedict."

He grumbled at me, but rose to his feet and padded out behind the girls.

Ash was sitting at one end of the bed, and me at the other. He made no motion to get up and move, so I smiled tentatively at him, wanting more than anything for him to stay.

"So, how are you doing?" he asked eventually, color rising in his cheeks.

I could feel the tension growing in the room, and I too blushed as I replied, "Fine. You?"

"Good. I think we probably need to talk about—"

"Hey." Hazel poked her head around the door, cutting Ash off. "Am I interrupting?" she asked, looking at us both.

"No," I replied too hastily. "It's fine."

"Tejus has guards looking for Julian," Hazel said. "They're out there now, searching around the borders." She came to sit down next to me on the bed. I shoved over to give her space, and she nestled her frame against me. There was something not quite right with Hazel—I could tell when my friend was out of sorts, and I'd never seen her look quite as miserable as this.

"Are you all right?" I asked her softly. "That's good news about Julian, right?"

"Yeah, it is. Sorry. I just feel a bit…" She trailed off. I got the impression that she didn't want to discuss anything further in front of Ash, which meant her problems were personal. And judging by the look on her face, they were Tejus-related. I left it alone.

"What about the borders?" I asked. "When are they lifting them?"

"That's part of the problem," she replied, her voice hardening. "The ministers have lifted the Hellswan borders, but not the Nevertide borders. They're saying that it's not a good idea right now—not when there's no emperor in place."

Ash muttered a profanity under his breath. "I knew it. This is so *typical*."

"It's the ministers," Hazel continued, "they're hesitating for some reason—and I don't think it really has anything to do with the lack of an emperor, but that's what they're saying. They said they'd discuss it with Tejus in private."

"That's convenient." Ash snorted with derision. I cast

him a warning glare.

"It's not Tejus. He wants the borders lifted." Hazel looked so lost all of a sudden. As much as I privately agreed with Ash—Tejus was king now, I doubted that much happened without his say-so—I wanted to comfort my friend more than start an argument about who was to blame. That would no doubt happen later.

"When did you last eat?" I asked Hazel, noticing how pale she looked.

"At the council meeting —I'm fine… I probably just need some sleep."

"I agree, but you should eat some more first," I replied firmly.

"We can go down to the kitchens," Ash said, standing up from the bed. "Come on."

* * *

Ash found us some leftovers, and we sat around a chopping board gnawing on cheese and bread. Seeing Ash back in the kitchen, and the ease with which he moved around the place, prompted me to ask what he'd be doing in Hellswan now—I hadn't seen him return to kitchen duties, but didn't know if it was a special holiday he'd been allowed or if it was a permanent thing.

He shrugged in reply. "Not sure. Usually when someone competes in the championships it changes how they're seen...but no one of common blood has ever gotten as far as I did—the sons and daughters of ministers, they're usually the ones who compete, then they become ministers too."

"Has anyone of common blood ever become a minister?" I asked, finding the term 'common' to describe Ash a bit hard to take. The social hierarchy in Nevertide did my head in—the fact that anyone could enter the kingship championships was impressively democratic, but we'd seen first-hand the bias of the ministers on point scoring.

"Not that I know of. Some must have, a long time ago. But the ministers...they like to keep their circle tight."

"Tell me about it," muttered Hazel darkly.

"Have you thought about asking Tejus? Asking to join his ministry?" I asked.

Ash nearly spat out his bread, and then roared with laughter. I glanced over at Hazel, but she looked as baffled by his outburst as I did.

"No!" he gasped out eventually. "No Hellswan would give me a job if I was the last sentry in Nevertide." He wiped tears of mirth from his cheeks. "No offense," he added after a moment, looking at Hazel.

"None taken," she muttered.

"Well, I don't see why," I continued. "You helped each other in the trials. He's no Jenus."

"No—I don't think the ministers here would take kindly to a kitchen boy joining their little secret meetings. I'd always be an outsider," he added more somberly.

That I understood, as unfair as it was.

"They'd be lucky to have you," I murmured, slightly embarrassed that Hazel was with us. She and I hadn't spoken about what had been going on with Ash and me, but judging from the small smile she was directing at the plate in front of her, she was starting to guess.

"Thanks, Shortie." Ash shot me a warm smile and reached for my hand under the table. I grasped it tightly, my heartbeat jumping a little while I tried to pretend, for Hazel's sake, that everything was perfectly normal.

Ash saw my unease, and the furtive glance I'd given Hazel. Giving me another squeeze, he released my hand.

"I'm going to call it a night. We'll go out early in the morning, look around the village. We'll have better luck than the guards there, the townspeople will be more inclined to talk to us."

"Good night then," I replied softly.

"'Night, Ash." Hazel yawned. She was looking a bit better color-wise, though obviously still tired, but I was glad I'd forced her to eat something.

"Are you *really* okay?" I asked her once Ash had left the room.

"I'm not sure. It's Tejus." She fiddled with a piece of bread, avoiding looking at me. "It's gotten… complicated somehow."

I knew that feeling.

"He's quite a… complicated character," I replied slowly, picking my words carefully.

"Yeah, you can say that again." She sighed. "I thought he might actually *like* me, but now I'm not sure. I don't even know why I care."

"Well, you obviously do… Think of your grandma, Sofia. I bet Derek was the last person in the world she thought she'd fall in love with."

Hazel smiled. "But I bet my grandpa was less of a total ass."

We shared a chuckle. Sofia might have a different opinion on that, given Derek's dark history.

It felt good to finally be spending alone time with Hazel. It had been too long. Though our evening was overshadowed by Julian's disappearance, I felt lighter than

I had in a long time.

"Just follow your heart." I nudged Hazel, giving her a cheesy grin. "Isn't that what your books tell you, anyway?"

Hazel rolled her eyes. "I don't think they'd be so keen on that mantra if they'd ever met Tejus... but you too, Ruby. Don't think I can't see what's been going on between you and Ash."

I blushed again, fiercely. Hazel smirked. "Don't worry, I don't need a play-by-play, just as long as he makes you happy... And I think he does."

"He does," I managed, my cheeks heating. *More than I care to admit.*

Julian

When I woke it was dark. After I'd met Queen Trina Seraq in the courtyard of her palace, she'd escorted me to a lavishly decorated room that I'd been locked in all day. I'd tried a million times to pry open the door, which wouldn't budge and eventually in frustration I'd given up. After that, I kept dropping off to sleep, not knowing what else I was supposed to do. There was one large window in the room, without bars or glass, but when I'd taken a chance and tried to climb out, I'd been faced with a sheer drop down to the ocean below, with nothing but air between me and the rocky shore.

I was well and truly trapped.

Now I sat up on the bed, shivering in the cold night air that came hurtling off the sea. Walking over to a large closet, I rifled through shelves of blankets and robes, picking the thickest and wrapping it around me. In front of the window, I'd been left a platter of exotic fruit, but after seeing the presence of nymphs in the castle, I wasn't so sure what I should or shouldn't be eating. I wouldn't be surprised if the brightly saturated food was poisonous, or at least contained hallucinatory properties.

No, thanks.

I paced up and down the room, more to keep warm than anything else.

I tried to work out why Queen Trina wanted me here. Clearly she was manipulating Benedict somehow, but I just couldn't understand *why*. When I'd seen him in the hallways of the castle that night he'd seemed to be acting alone, but what I'd assumed was sleepwalking was probably some spell or hypnotism—and maybe Queen Trina was behind it all. The last thing I'd seen before blacking out and being dragged away was Ruby falling to the floor with Benedict standing over her, completely motionless, as if he didn't even recognize her. I felt sick when I recalled the image, not knowing whether she was alive or dead. But why had Queen Trina taken me? She could have just knocked me out…unless I'd seen too much already.

I wished I'd paid more attention to Benedict when he'd started to behave oddly—the pale face, complaining of never sleeping, all starting the night we'd found that narrow passage…I should have listened. I'd been so preoccupied with finding a way out of Nevertide, and the stupid Hell Rakers group, that I'd ignored what was right in front of me.

It suddenly occurred to me that the others could already be out of Nevertide by now—the trials were over, there wouldn't be anything stopping them from lowering the borders.

They wouldn't leave without you, a small voice reassured me. But I knew it wasn't true—we would have left without Hazel the first time if Jenus hadn't intervened. They would leave, but I knew without a doubt that my parents and GASP would come back to find me…if they could.

A soft knock on the door broke my train of thought.

"Who's there?" I called, rushing over to the door.

"Can I come in?" asked a soft, feminine voice. The nymph.

"It's locked," I retorted, returning to the bed in frustration. She wouldn't be any help. I heard her giggle from behind the door, and then the heavy clunks of locks turning. The door swung open.

"Magic!" she exclaimed, pirouetting in the doorway. She looked as lovely as before—the wild leaves and flowers entwined in her hair, the soft glowing aura around her, and the bizarre dress of foliage doing nothing to detract from the enchanting violet eyes that peered down at me.

"I've got a lovely surprise for you." She smiled, dancing into the room. "The queen requests your company—are you dressed well?"

I looked down at my blanket.

"Uh…wait," I replied, taking one of the robes from the closet and throwing it over my clothes.

"That *does* look dashing." She giggled again. "You're a vision in purple!"

I looked down at the robe. It was black.

"Thanks," I muttered. I suppose it didn't really matter what color she thought I was wearing, but I was unaccountably pleased that she liked my outfit. I supposed it *did* look quite good. Dignified.

"The queen likes things to look nice. Everyone should be like that." She smiled, beckoning me toward the hallway outside the room. "Don't you think? There's so much ugliness in the universe…I like things to look nice too."

"Me too," I replied, realizing that it was so true. I'd never given it much thought, but the nymph was right— why shouldn't things be beautiful?

We walked along the hallway, and I admired the polished marble floor and the Grecian-looking arches that swept over us. The nymph almost seemed to float along the corridor in her gracefulness.

"Do you like the palace?" I asked.

"Oh, yes!" she replied, laughing. "I love to play here…all my friends do. Not many people in Nevertide like us." She pulled a face at me. "But Queen Trina isn't like that, she loves to dance and drink with us. You should come to one of our parties, human boy, you'd have so much fun!"

"I'd like that," I found myself replying. "How often do you have them?"

"Oh, all the time. Especially when the queen has guests. Not everyone agrees with her lifestyle, so she keeps it quite private. Only specially chosen people can join us. King Tejus liked us! We had such fun when he was here." She giggled, stroking the flowers in her hair. I found myself laughing too, hoping that I'd be here long enough to attend one of the parties—it would be a shame to waste the opportunity while I was in Nevertide.

"King Tejus was my favorite," the nymph sighed. "He was such a gentleman—so devoted to the queen. Not like her father...he hated us being here, such a sour man." She shook her pretty head in displeasure. "He hated to dance."

"He sounds awful," I agreed.

"Listen!" the nymph exclaimed, pointing to the sky.

"What?" I whispered back after a moment, not hearing anything.

"The moon! Can't you hear it sing? It sounds so beautiful...I wonder what it sings about?"

I shook my head in amazement. I had no idea. I hadn't even known that the moon *did* sing.

The nymph continued to dance along the corridor, her faint glow lighting up the darkened passage.

"We're here." She turned to me suddenly, gesturing to a large white-washed wooden door. "The queen awaits you. Be nice to her, human boy. We all love her very much."

I opened my mouth to ask if I should knock, but the nymph seemed to have vanished into thin air. I looked around wildly, crushed by her abrupt absence.

Without warning, the door in front of me opened and Queen Trina stood before me.

"Hello." I smiled at her.

"Oh, for goodness' sake." She turned away from me. "Didn't you eat the food I gave you?"

I didn't know what food she was talking about. I looked around the rest of the room, seeing if the nymph was hiding somewhere, but she was truly gone.

"I'm sorry to disturb you," I said as politely as I could, "but have you seen—"

"A pretty maiden dressed in leaves?" came the acerbic reply. "No. Drink this."

Queen Trina shoved a cup of steaming liquid under my nose—it stank, and I took a step back.

"Drink it," she ordered. "It's an herb. It cancels out the effects of the nymphs."

She shoved it with more force toward me, and tentatively I took a sip. It didn't taste as bad as it smelled, thankfully.

"All of it," she barked.

I drank down the liquid… *Oh, damn.* As the fog lifted, an unpleasant clarity asserted itself. "Why do you keep those…*things* around?" I seethed. "If she'd asked me to jump off a cliff I would have!"

"Watch your tongue," she hissed at me. "And sit."

She gestured to a chair placed in front of a large desk,

made entirely of a bright blue stone that seemed to be *alive* somehow, with light dancing and moving within it.

"What am I doing here?" I asked, not wanting to give her the satisfaction of seeing me marvel at the grandeur of her office.

"I told you—you were getting in the way of my plans," she replied airily.

"And those *plans* are?"

"Never you mind. They don't concern you."

"But they concern my friend, Benedict—right? Do you know he's only fourteen? He's a *kid*!" I wanted to punch something. I felt so helpless here, letting her do God knew what with Benedict and the rest of my friends.

"He is fine," she retorted. "And he will continue to be fine. He has a benevolent and kind master now; he is incredibly lucky."

"I have no idea what you're talking about," I spat.

"Of course you don't. For good reason." She smiled with saccharine sweetness. "So—Julian. Let us discuss the options you have before you. You will find that I'm a very generous jailor…as long as you are willing to cooperate, of course."

I didn't bother answering her, and I didn't feel like being very *cooperative*.

"Very well." She smirked, evidently finding my attitude amusing. "You have two choices. You may reside in the dungeons down below this castle—rather grim, and cold this time of year." She mock-shivered. "Or you are welcome to enjoy my lavish playground, and all the wonders that it has to offer."

I remained silent, waiting for the catch. This wasn't my first kidnapping.

"On the condition that you always remain under the watch of a nymph." Her eyes glinted with victory. "It appears to me that you rather *enjoy* their company, do you not?"

I considered my options with a heavy heart.

I knew without a doubt that the more pleasant of the two alternatives would be to spend my days in the castle with the company of the nymphs—but I also knew that it would be the quickest way for me to forget my friends, to abandon any hope of trying to escape…and I couldn't imagine it would be that long before I forgot my own name. I closed my eyes, not wanting to see the mocking smile of Queen Trina sitting before me.

It was no choice at all.

"The dungeons," I whispered.

She laughed loudly. "My! You've got more courage than

I gave you credit for, human. It's a good thing I took you out of Hellswan when I did! So be it then," she continued. "The dungeons it is. A wise choice, though I doubt you'll live long enough to benefit from it. As I said, it gets terribly cold down there…and endless days and nights spent in pitch darkness, not knowing when dawn has risen or the sun has set? It does curious things to the mind, my dear. Very curious."

I jumped up from the chair and lunged toward her, my hands outstretched. I wanted to strangle her. Rip her limb from limb if I'd had claws - completely destroy her.

As soon as my fingers brushed the wool of her blue cloak, she stepped backward and a lightning bolt of excruciating pain ricocheted through my head. I screamed, falling to the ground in a crumpled heap, my body withering in pain. My efforts were pitiful.

The last thing I heard before passing out completely was the delighted, girlish laughter of Queen Trina Seraq.

She thinks this is all a game.

Benedict

I groaned as a gust of cold air numbed my face and hands. Still believing I was in bed, I turned over in half-sleep, trying to locate my blanket. Instead of the soft wool I hoped to find, my fingers touched damp sand.

This isn't right.

Icy-cold realization washed over me, and I sat up abruptly. In the light of the moon I could recognize the malformed humps and vertical jutting plains of the Viking graveyard, and a sickening green light erupting from the ground a few yards ahead. Dread clenched my gut as I rose to my feet, dully putting one step in front of the other as my body drew me toward the light. Once again I felt like someone's puppet, animated by their strings, completely out of control of my own body and mind. I couldn't even understand how I'd gotten here. When I went to bed I had made sure that I locked my door – and even wedged a chair beneath the door handle. I couldn't remember waking up and moving through the castle, or leaving the grounds through the portcullis. Which could only mean that I was losing more time—experiencing more blank spots where I could have been doing *anything*, and I wouldn't know.

That thought terrified me more than the eerie light that beckoned up ahead.

I followed, my feet stumbling over the uneven earth, but determined to reach my destination. With each step I took, I could feel the power of the light growing stronger—not just the light's intensity, but the force I could feel coming off it, drifting over to me in waves.

Soon I no longer wanted to turn back. Everything in me wanted to see what lay beneath the earth, to discover what the green light promised.

I passed a hole in the ground, a bright shard of light pouring out of it and reaching up into the sky. I thought that something must have fallen through, an animal perhaps, or maybe it was just a natural pothole. I tried to peer down it, but the light was too bright—and still I was being pulled forward, to another spill of light ahead.

A yard from the hole, the earth dipped down low, tree roots exposed in the soil landslide. In the glow of the light they looked like a mass of sprawling limbs, and I hurried past them into a stone passage. The light was bright here, but less intense, so I could make my way along the narrow path easily. The walls on either side of me were made of large stone blocks, and on each I could see strange engravings—a bit like the runes on the Viking relics, but different somehow, like they held power. Like they were *alive*, not just carved shapes.

As I made my way along the passage, I could hear voices droning—a low, steady hum that came from repetition of a prayer or mantra, over and over again. I couldn't make out what the voices were saying, but I knew they were sentry voices or human, not the strange whisperings that I'd been hearing in the castle, though they called to me in the same way.

I stepped out of the passage, into a small room. In the middle was a large stone shape where the green glow was strongest, and surrounding it, all dressed in black robes, were about a dozen sentries. Their hoods were worn low over their faces, so I couldn't recognize any of them.

They ignored me, continuing to chant, but among them

I felt a strange sense of well-being, like I was in exactly the place I was meant to be—with people who *understood*, who knew about the stones, the whisperings and everything else that had been happening to me since I came to Nevertide.

I moved closer to the table. The chanting sentries didn't move from the circular stance, allowing me to reach out and touch the smooth, warm slab that formed the top of the table. My eyes adjusted to the brightness of the light, and I could see that the same runes were carved here too, and it was these patterns and shapes that the light spilled out from.

My body started to feel as if it was vibrating, humming with energy. A moment later I realized that it was coming from my trouser pocket. I reached my hand down, and, slipping my fingers inside the rough cotton of my jeans, I felt the stone Hazel had given me. It was almost too hot to touch, and when I pulled it out, it glowed even brighter than the runes.

I stood still, stupefied, the stone in my outstretched palm, the hot searing of my skin not seeming to matter, my eyes darting from the stone to the table.

The droning of the ministers stopped.

A woman's voice spoke out, one that I recognized.

"Will you not do your duty, Benedict of Hellswan? You

are the chosen one. The creature from another dimension, called forth to save us, to set us free. So it is written, so it shall be."

Yes!

More than anything, I wanted to do my duty—to fulfill my purpose.

The vibrating of the stone increased, shuddering through my body. I knew what I must do—the very thing that I'd been waiting to do since I'd first heard the whispers and seen the unearthly swirls on the wall in the castle. Slowly I placed the stone down on the table and watched, open-mouthed, as it rolled of its own accord into the center and then placed itself into a small divot, enclosing it so perfectly that it looked like the stone had always been there.

I looked over at the female sentry who had spoken, and watched as she slowly removed the hood from her face. I smiled as I met the almond-shaped eyes of Queen Trina Seraq.

I wanted to call out, to speak to her once again, but the room shifted, blurring and jolting…

No, wait!

I grasped the slab of the table, trying to hold onto reality a moment longer, but the room was already spinning, becoming a blur of robed figures and the eyes of Queen Trina growing larger and larger until everything went black.

Hazel

When I first woke, I thought that I'd completely misjudged the time—outside the window, the sky was still dark, and it took me a moment to realize that it *was* in fact morning, but an almost black rolling blanket of cloud had covered the sun. I wrapped my robe round me more tightly, shivering. It looked ominous—thunder clattered against the windows, and it seemed that the whole of Nevertide was covered in a bleak misery.

I went to get washed and dressed, taking my time so that I could delay coming face-to-face with Tejus. A hot bath helped, and I stayed submerged in the water till my skin became wrinkly and I half-worried that I'd pass out from the heat.

When I entered the living room, I found Tejus sitting on one of the sofas, with Lucifer purring around his legs for attention.

Tejus turned in my direction, briefly nodding 'hello' before returning his attention to the storms outside.

"What's going on with the weather?" I asked, attempting to break the silence. Last night I'd vowed that today I'd ask to move down to the human quarters—it would be easier on us both, and until we were allowed to leave Nevertide it was probably best I stayed away from Tejus.

"I've never seen it like this," he murmured. He looked concerned, and I noticed dark shadows under his eyes as if he hadn't gotten much sleep. I wondered if the kingly duties were already getting to him, but it occurred to me that other than in made-up scenarios in our mind-melds, I'd never actually seen Tejus relaxed or at ease.

I moved to sit opposite him on the sofa, thinking that now was a good a time as any to discuss my sleeping arrangements.

"I was thinking that I might move my things down to the human quarters—until we move out. I'm sure you'd be happy to get some privacy."

"What are you talking about?" he replied in irritation.

"Moving downstairs. Today," I repeated.

"No."

His jaw clenched in resolution, and he turned away from me.

"Okay, well, I was being polite," I retorted. "You're no longer my jailor. I'm going to stay downstairs."

He rose from the sofa, glaring at me.

"Do you think that because my brother isn't here, you're *safe*?" he growled. "I am king now, Hazel. If anyone would seek to harm me, and there are plenty who would, *you* are the person they would target first—are you so blind?"

"Who is going to harm you?" I exploded in exasperation. "I just want to *leave,* Tejus—please!"

My desperation was getting the better of me. I wanted the dignity of leaving on my own terms, but I didn't know how to say that without letting him know how much he was starting to hurt me.

"If I knew that, I wouldn't be concerned," he bit out. "Why are you so desperate to leave? Anything you want or need is yours here."

No, it's not.

I swallowed. "I just want to get out of your way, that's

all."

"I do not want that," he replied quietly. "Hazel, I—"

The door to his living quarters thundered with a loud knock.

Are you kidding me?

I wanted to scream. It seemed that every time Tejus was about to tell me something, every time we were about to attempt a meaningful conversation, someone would interrupt.

"Enter," he called out. I was slightly mollified by the fact that he sounded as pissed off as I did by the interruption.

"The ministers are ready for you, your Highness." A man bowed at the doorway and left. Tejus walked swiftly to his room, leaving the door open as he walked over to the bed that evidently hadn't been slept in and threw off his shirt. I could see the faint glow of the torchlight bouncing off the muscles of his bare back, and I quickly averted my eyes.

"Unless the matter is closed, we can discuss this when I return," he called out from his room.

"Are you going to talk about the borders?" I asked.

"Yes. That's why I called the meeting."

"Will you ask about Julian?" I added.

"Yes."

He emerged from his room in a fresh shirt, tying back his hair as he strode toward the door.

"Am I going to have to lock you in?" he asked, his face impassive, but I thought I could detect a faint trace of humor in his tone.

"You're joking."

"Don't tempt me, Hazel, because I will."

With that, he left the room. Shutting, but not locking, the door behind him. I collapsed on the sofa.

I didn't understand why he felt I was under such threat. The castle seemed well secured for the most part, and no harm had come to the rest of the humans—besides Julian, who I suspected had left voluntarily. Was it that he worried I would be a prime target, that the rest of Nevertide was as confused as I was about our relationship? I recalled what the servant girl had been saying before the coronation, wondering whether I was considering *staying* with Tejus after the trials. How strange was it, in the terms of Nevertide customs, that I was staying with their king? The thought made me flush with embarrassment...and gave me another reason to relocate downstairs.

I also hated not knowing what was going on with the ministers, and why they seemed so reluctant to open one border but not the other. I wondered if Tejus would tell me the truth behind their reasons—evidently he was an expert at keeping secrets, and Queen Trina popped into my mind...and the way I'd found out about their relationship by overhearing an argument; how he hadn't told me about anything about my attempted kidnapper when he had known full well that it was her all along.

I shot up from the sofa, determined to get to the bottom of at least *one* of the mysteries at Hellswan castle. If I hurried, I wouldn't miss much of the meeting. I only hoped that it would be taking place in the same room as last time, otherwise I'd waste hours trying to find them.

* * *

I'd located the meeting room, but stood back behind a corner of the hallway, avoiding being seen by the two guards placed at the door. They hadn't been there last time, and it confirmed my suspicions that the ministers had something to hide—they seemed to be going to a lot of trouble to sort out what I'd initially assumed would be a quick sentry mind-trick.

The presence of the guards was a problem. Hopefully there would be another way in, but I couldn't remember the layout of the room that well. Beyond the gray stone walls there was little to set it apart from the other rooms in the castle, with the exception of the oil paintings…which, on the furthest wall, had hung above wooden paneling – and I was sure I'd seen the outline of a door. *That was it.*

Now I just needed to find the right wall, which I assumed would be at the other end of the hallway. Squaring my shoulders, I stepped out from behind my hiding spot and strode purposefully along the wide corridor. The guards barely looked up at me, and I passed by them without a word being uttered between us. When I reached the end of the hallway, I swerved left and pushed open the first door I came to.

It opened into an empty office, which smelt musty with age. There was a dark oak desk, and some moldy-looking books on shelves, but other than that it was bare. I was relieved at the sight of a wooden door that would open onto the meeting chamber. I moved closer, and pressed my cheek against the cold surface. I could hear soft mutterings coming from within—but I needed to open it if I was going to make out what they were actually saying.

Very gently, I pushed against the door and held my breath, praying that it wouldn't creak with age. To my relief, it softly gave way by less than an inch into the chamber with only a small click of the latch.

I could hear voices immediately, but could only see a few ministers with their backs toward me. I looked around for Tejus, but he must have been on the other side of the table, facing the main entrance.

Soon I heard his voice, low and menacing, cutting through the muttering of the ministers.

"You have still failed to give me a sufficient explanation, Lithan. As I told you before, the situation is dire. I want the humans out of my sight, the sooner the better."

The ministers went silent.

I felt the same painful jolt I'd felt at the last meeting, hearing once again how easily he dismissed us all—how easily he dismissed *me*. And yet, a moment ago, he had been telling me that I couldn't leave his living quarters... Something didn't add up. Either he was saying hurtful things in order to get his way with the ministers—but he was king, why wouldn't they do what he commanded anyway? Why did he feel he needed to prove his dislike of us?—or he truly wanted us gone as quickly as possible, but wanted to keep a careful watch over me in the meantime. It made no sense to me.

"Your Highness, the situation is... *sensitive*. We are not entirely sure what we are dealing with here," another minister replied, their voice taut with anxiety.

"Try to explain it, then," Tejus replied curtly. I could tell that he was close to losing his temper, but trying to rein it in, probably for the sake of propriety… though he'd never struck me as someone who was willing to bow to rules.

"The fact is, your Highness, that we simply can't open up the borders—they are held too strong!" a squeaky voice replied, and I recognized it as Qentos, the most insipid minister of the lot.

"Really, Qentos? That surprises me—as you told me that it was *you* who put them up," Tejus replied.

"Your father, the late emperor—rest his soul—commanded us to tell you that falsehood on his death bed. He, and we, believed he would soon regain his strength. He swore he would regain control of the borders…but it was not to be."

Huh? What?

If the ministers weren't keeping the borders up, then who was?

"On pain of death, Lithan, you will tell me *right now* who exactly has control of the borders." Tejus's voice was deadly. I almost pitied Lithan, and could hear the collective intake of breath at Tejus's threat. I didn't believe it was an empty one—and neither did they.

"We believe it is what we know as 'the entity'…an aged force. Long before our time, it was this *creature* who created the sentries, your highness—it ruled us once, and rules us still."

The room was silent.

"I ask you for an answer, Lithan, and you tell me a ghost story?" Tejus mocked.

"It is no story, your highness. We wish that it was. Your late father had control over this creature, as all emperors before him did…but with no emperor, the creature grows stronger."

Creature?

Was this some huge lie they were concocting to defy him in some way? But for what purpose? And of all the lies to tell…this seemed about as far-fetched as it got.

"I see," Tejus replied, his voice heavy with disdain. "And how, pray tell, did my father *control* this creature?"

"There are stones, their power beyond our comprehension, buried deep within the walls of this castle. Hellswan has been the seat of the emperor for generations. We hoped, as we always have, that the Emperor would remain a Hellswan, and continue to reside here. That way, the stones were always under the guard of the emperor, never left unattended, until now."

Lithan's story sent shivers running through my body.

Stones.

I thought of the one I had taken from the Hellswan sword, its power incredible, so much so that it gave me the sentry True Sight. Was there a connection there? Was the stone one of those that was meant to be buried within the castle, controlling some *entity*?

"Do you know the location of these stones?" Tejus asked, his disbelief still evident in his tone.

"We do not." Lithan sighed. "The location of the stones has been lost to us over the years. Many of our documents have been damaged or lost—Nevertide hasn't faced a threat in over a century. I assume those before us became rather slack in their duties."

"As, it seems, did you."

"And we apologize most humbly, your highness," Lithan countered.

"So what use would an emperor be if you don't know where the stones are?" Tejus questioned.

The ministers started to whisper amongst themselves. A crash thundered across the room, silencing them all. I jumped from my crouched position, thankfully falling away from the door. Scrambling back up, I couldn't see what had happened, but I imagined that Tejus had just slammed his fist down on the table.

There goes the propriety, I thought sarcastically. But in fairness, I was close to losing my temper too—the ministers seemed to know next to nothing that would be of help, and yet what little they *did* know, they were reluctant to share.

"There...there is a book," Qentos's reedy voice stuttered, "that only the emperor is privy to by a decree of ancient law. It cannot be read by another—only by he who is chosen from among his people to rule all the kingdoms...but we believe that this book tells of the location of the stones."

"This is utterly ridiculous—an invisible entity, magic stones of unprecedented power, and a book that only an emperor can read," Tejus announced in barely concealed fury. "Have you any proof whatsoever that this being exists?"

"Only the outer Nevertide boundaries, your highness. We have been trying to lower them, with all the ministers of the six kingdoms, and we can't."

I slumped back against the wall. I had heard enough. Enough to believe that the ministers weren't making this up—the fear in their voices was real enough, even if what they were saying sounded utterly implausible.

I wished, not for the first time, that GASP were here. My mom and dad would have known what to do, and Corrine would no doubt have had the stupid borders lifted without much difficulty. The only thing I knew for sure was that I needed to find my brother and retrieve the stone. I wasn't sure whether or not it was the same thing as the entity stones, but I couldn't be too careful.

Ruby

The skies had been rumbling overhead all morning. It was a depressing sight, and though it was just storm clouds, something about their looming presence made me feel uneasy. As we made our way toward Hellswan village, I kept reminding myself that being out of the castle for the morning made a nice change, and I wanted to make the most of it, despite frequent gusts of wind blowing debris in our path and the cobbled streets being almost completely deserted.

Ash took my hand, offering reassurance. Mine closed over his tightly. For once I wasn't worried what my friends might think of our open display of affection. Benedict, who was walking with us, saw, but only rolled his eyes and tutted—something he would have done whether Ash was a human, a sentry, or an alien from outer space. Regardless of our displeased audience, I felt lighter all of a sudden, pleased to have more evidence that Ash's feelings might match my own.

"It's the next house along," Ash called out over the wind. Our first stop was an old friend of his father's, who Ash claimed was about as nosy and interfering as they came...the perfect place to start our search.

Ash banged on the door of the small wooden lean-to. It seemed to shake the entire foundation, and I tugged at him to stop, worried we'd annoy the man before we set foot in his home.

"Don't worry." Ash grinned. "He's pretty deaf."

A moment later, the door swung open, and a tall, grim-looking man who must have been over ninety years old stood with a lantern swinging from his hand.

"Ashbik!" he grumbled. "Haven't seen you in an age. Too good for us now, are you?"

Ash laughed. "Stand aside—let us in, old man."

Still grumbling, the man eyed Benedict and me closely, and just when I thought he was going to slam the door in our faces, he stood aside to let us in.

"Sit down," he said, gesturing at battered old chairs that surrounded a small fire. We did as we were told.

Ash waited till the man sat down before beginning to talk.

"Otso, we've lost a friend of ours—a human boy. We think he may have left the castle on his own after the trials finished. I was wondering if you'd seen him, or heard anything?" Ash asked.

The old man shook his head.

"No human has passed this way. And no human ought!" He turned to glare at Benedict and me. "There are omens starting, lad," he continued. "Dark skies, dark deeds. Your human is better off in the woods with the beasties than he is near that castle, mark my words."

Ash shook his head slightly at Benedict and me, a warning not to take the man too seriously. But I couldn't help but be affected by Otso's words. Whether he was nutty or not, I couldn't deny that I felt the same misgivings about Hellswan.

"You, boy," the man barked at Benedict. "You've seen the signs—I can see it written on your face…the whispers have marked you, boy, but I can see!"

Benedict stood up, his face white.

"I'm going to wait outside," he muttered to me.

"I'll join you," I replied hastily, rising from my chair. Anything to get away from the old man—he might have been an old friend of Ash's father, but he was also certifiably insane.

We stood outside in the cold, huddled together at the side of the old man's house, waiting for Ash to finish up.

"Ignore Otso," I said, noticing that Benedict still looked uncomfortable. "He's obviously just a batty old man."

"Yeah, I know," Benedict replied weakly. I put my arm around him, glancing toward the front door with impatience. Clearly the man knew nothing about Julian's whereabouts, and I doubted Ash would get anything useful out of him.

Ash emerged a few moments later, looking irritated.

"Hey." Benedict and I hurried toward him. "Anything remotely helpful?" I asked.

"Nope. He's going batty. I'm actually quite worried about him..." Ash ran his hand through his hair in agitation. "He used to be a great guy. Sorry about that, Benedict."

"Don't worry about it." Benedict shook off the apology. "Not your fault."

We continued to walk over the cobblestones, following the main street that ran the length of the village. Stall frames were set up on either side of us, positioned in front of misshapen houses and barns. I imagined that usually this was a lively street and the main trade location of Hellswan, but today it was completely empty. The only noises were the occasional window shutter banging in the wind, and the odd whicker of an unhappy bull-horse.

"Hey, Ash!" a voice called out in the empty street. All three of us looked around, but couldn't see a soul.

"Up here!" An attractive red-headed girl was peering out of a top floor window, waving down at us. "I just wanted to say that I'm sorry you didn't make king. I was rooting for you, we all were."

Ash waved back. "Thanks, Gladys, I appreciate it."

"You're ten times the man that Hellswan swine is," she called back merrily.

Ash nodded, smiling grimly. "Have you seen a human pass this way?" he added before she could shut the window.

"No. No humans this way. You better get back to the castle as well, Ash." She looked toward the dark black cloud and shook her head. "Nothing good can come of this."

Geez. It's just a storm.

The sentries were certainly a superstitious lot. In so many ways being in Nevertide was like stepping back in time to a little medieval village, and while sometimes I could find that strangely charming, most of the time I found it unbearably frustrating—and this 'bad omen' stuff was starting to wear a bit thin.

The woman closed the windows, and we carried on.

"Where to now?" I asked Ash, hoping he had some better ideas up his sleeve.

"The local witch," he replied with a smile.

What?

"Really, Nevertide has witches?" I asked.

"She's not an actual witch. I just mean that she's good with herbal remedies and stuff—it's the nickname we give her in the village," Ash explained.

"Oh." That was disappointing. It would have been comforting to meet a member of a species I was actually familiar with here in this dark land.

We walked to the end of the village, where the houses started to peter out and give way to miles of hills and meadows in the distance. I looked around for a trinket-covered hovel, but all I could see was a smart stone house, with a freshly painted sign reading 'Abelle's Apothecary' flapping in the wind.

We trudged up the stone steps and Ash knocked on the door. We waited a while, but eventually it opened, revealing a smiling woman who I guessed was in her mid-forties. For a sentry she was quite short, only a head taller than me, with a voluptuous figure.

"Ashbik!" she cried, embracing him warmly. "And you've brought friends—I recognize you from the trials." She smiled at me.

"Hello, I'm Ruby. This is Benedict."

"I'm Abelle. Come on in." She ushered us all inside, and I was instantly hit by a fragrant warmth that smelt of cedar wood. The front room looked like a greenhouse, with potted plants covering every available surface and dried herbs hanging from the ceiling by twine.

"I haven't seen you in so long, Ash." She ruffled his hair. "I was so proud of you in the trials—you've given us all hope. Things have been stagnant here for too long – not enough crops, not enough to trade," she gesticulated extravagantly, "everyone living hand to mouth these days. It's not a good time. Let us hope a change is upon us…but you haven't come for my opinion on the state of Nevertide. To what do I owe the pleasure?" she asked, snapping some dead leaves off a nearby plant and tucking them into her apron.

"We're actually looking for a friend of ours—a human. Dark hair, brown eyes. He would have perhaps come this way after the trials. Have you seen anything?" Ash asked.

The woman looked worried. "No, I haven't. I'm sorry. Why would he leave the castle on his own? It's dangerous for a human. Times like these..." She trailed off into silence.

"We don't really know," I replied. "We think he got impatient waiting for the borders to come down, and wanted to find a break in the barriers himself."

"Ah." She nodded. "The barriers. Of course." She looked perturbed for a few moments, but before I could press her on why, she beamed at us again. "I'm sorry I can't help, but I will keep an eye out. I hope you find your friend."

I felt that she genuinely meant it, and aside from Ash and Jenney, Abelle was the first sentry I'd instantly warmed to.

She turned to look at me, her bright eyes boring into mine, as if searching for the answer to some unspoken question. Seeming satisfied with what she saw, she abruptly broke the connection and turned to Ash. I felt a bit woozy, and wondered if Abelle had performed some ultra-light mind-meld on me...

"Ash, why don't you and Benedict fetch some of the bread I baked last night? It's in the pantry, you know the way. I made too much. You can take it back with you."

Ash looked momentarily confused, but he nodded. "Thanks… um, come on, Benedict."

The two of them left the room, Ash leading the way to the pantry.

"What did you just do to me?" I asked once they were out of earshot.

"Sorry," she replied in a whisper, sounding sincere. "It's just a little energy check—people's energy can sort of be *read*, if you know what to look for. Please understand, Ash is like a son to me. And I'm worried about him…and what he's going to do next."

"What do you mean?" I asked.

"I saw Queen Trina at the trials, rooting for him…and it was good that she did, but it was also unusual. There are rumors about the queen, some unsavory enough for me to worry." She paused, trying to choose her words carefully. "I could be completely wrong—really, take everything I say with a pinch of salt—but will you watch out for Ash? Especially if the queen reappears on the scene…" She trailed off as we heard footsteps ascending the staircase.

"Of course," I reassured her.

Ash and Benedict reappeared empty-handed.

"Abelle, I'm really sorry. I couldn't find anything," Ash

announced.

"Couldn't you?" Abelle feigned surprise. "Maybe I gave it all away already—I'm so sorry."

"Don't worry about it," replied Ash with a dawning suspicion. He turned to me, but I kept my expression as innocent as possible.

We left her house soon after, with Abelle's warning still ringing in my ears. I had been so pleased by Queen Trina's support of Ash I'd never thought to question it other than assuming that she clearly had a dislike of Tejus...but in Nevertide, hating a Hellswan seemed to be practically a birthright. I'd never stopped to think that Queen Trina might have other, more sinister, motives.

We walked back the way we'd come, all of us a little downhearted that we'd been unable to discover anything of use. The winds hadn't let up, and if anything seemed to be increasing in their intensity.

As we passed a crumbling barn near the old man's house, I paused. It could have been the wind, but I could have sworn that I could hear someone crying from within. I tugged on Ash's hand, nodding toward the barn. All three of us were silent, and the distinct sound of wailing carried across the wind.

We tentatively approached the barn, and I knocked on

the broken door.

"Hello?" I called out. "Is someone there?"

No reply. I looked at Ash and Benedict, and we crossed the threshold.

It was gloomy in the barn, but soon my eyes adjusted and I could see a small boy on the hay-strewn floor, crying over the body of a slain goat-like creature, with four horns instead of two and six legs instead of four.

"Are you okay?" I rushed over to the boy, placing my hands on his shoulders. He turned his tear-stained and dirty face up toward me.

"He's dead!" the boy cried. "He was my *friend,* and someone *killed* him." He continued to cry with heart-wrenching sobs, and I looked helplessly back at Ash and Benedict. Ash shrugged awkwardly. But Benedict was staring at the wall, his eyes bulging. I followed his gaze, and my stomach lurched.

On the wall a crude shape had been drawn in what I assumed was the goat's blood. Its lines were sharp, vicious-looking, as if the shape was meant to strike fear in the heart of its observer. I didn't know what it meant, and had never seen anything like it before; the image depicted an upside-down triangle with a thick line struck through the middle of it, and entwined round that line was another, like a snake. At the bottom of the thick line there was a semi-circle with dashes rising from it—a sunset, perhaps.

"Have you seen this before?" I breathed to Ash.

"Never."

"Is it a…rune or something?"

"No idea," he replied quietly.

I looked over at Benedict, who hadn't taken his eyes off the shape on the wall. He looked absolutely terrified, and I racked my brains to think of something to say that might calm him.

"You know, everyone round here is really displeased that Tejus won the trials…it's probably just some medieval vandalism," I said, shrugging it off.

"Did you see who did this?" Ash asked the boy, but he just shook his head and continued to cry into the fur of the dead animal.

"Does the sign mean anything to you?" I asked, more gently.

He shook his head again. "I don't know what that is, but I know it's…*evil!*" he burst out.

Benedict looked even more terrified at the boy's assessment, so I reached for his hand, pulling him out of the barn.

"Ash, we need to go, come on."

I felt sorry for the crying boy, but there was nothing more we could do—and my priority was Benedict. It looked like today had been too much for him: first the old man yelling at him about strange whispers and evil omens, and now dead goats and blood splashed on crumbling barns. And I had been warned about Queen Trina getting too close to Ash. Just when I'd thought Nevertide couldn't get any stranger, it managed once again to prove me wrong.

I couldn't wait to get out of here.

Wherever you are, Mom and Dad… please hurry up and find us.

Hazel

I sat in the ministers' office for a while, digesting what I'd heard. None of it made sense to me—the mysterious 'entity', the stones locked away in the depths of the castle, or the fact that it had all been kept a secret from the people of Nevertide, for the emperor only to know…and I wondered how much Tejus's father had known, if the ministers were so vague on the matter. But perhaps this was all revealed in the mysterious book Qentos had spoken about.

When my head stopped spinning, I left the office with a dull headache, but determined to tell the others what I'd heard. Maybe together we could make better sense of the ministers' discussion. It was also imperative that I got the stone off Benedict—if it *was* one of the stones that controlled the power of the entity, then I certainly didn't want it anywhere near my brother.

Cautiously, I opened the door of the ministers' office, and, seeing that the coast was clear, I let myself out and quietly shut the door behind me. I hurried along the empty hallways till I entered the human quarters.

Two guards were stationed outside, but they waved me through.

Ruby and Ash were sitting on the sofas with Jenney. Ruby waved me over, her face pale and drawn.

"Is everything okay?" I asked, looking around at the deserted room. Normally it was full to the brim with kids. "Where is everyone?"

"They're all eating in the kitchen," Ruby replied, smiling wryly. "It should give us at least an hour of peace and quiet."

"Is Benedict there too?" I wanted to speak to him about the stone in private, before I told the others about what I'd overheard.

"No, he's gone to bed already. We had a weird day. I think he took it quite hard." Ruby proceeded to tell me about the villagers they'd met and the horrible rune-type image they'd seen on the wall of the barn.

"That sounds awful," I exhaled. Ruby was right. Things in Nevertide were getting stranger. "Will you draw me the image you saw?" I asked. "I want to see if Tejus recognizes it."

We found a pencil and paper in one of the old chests in the living quarters, and Ruby sketched out the image. It looked strange on paper, and I was glad that I'd not been the one to see it painted out in blood—no wonder Benedict had wanted to forget today in sleep.

After I'd put the paper in my pocket, I told them what I'd overheard at the meeting, only leaving out the comments Tejus had made about wanting the humans out of here; Ruby would have been upset, and it served no purpose.

"It sounds like a load of manure to me," Ash commented when I'd finished. "Just another excuse from the ministers not to do the right thing and lower the borders...I've never even heard a mention of this 'entity'. Don't you think someone would know *something* about it if it were true?"

"I don't know," I replied. "They sounded serious—and pretty scared."

"It's so far-fetched," Ruby countered. "If there was

some...*thing* in the castle, some malevolent evil or whatever, don't you think we'd have felt it by now?"

I was getting frustrated with their refusal to take what I was saying seriously. I knew it sounded far-fetched, but if either of them had overheard what I had this afternoon, they would think twice before dismissing it out of hand. And it wasn't like Ruby to act like this—she questioned everything always, but rarely dismissed something so easily.

"I don't know," I sighed, "but don't you think it's a bit strange that the ministers can't lower the borders at all? What other reason could they possibly have for keeping them up?"

Ash laughed. "How about the Imperial trials? Don't you think an entire room of humans would come in handy for Tejus when he competes for those? Remember the ministers here have a vested interest in Tejus becoming emperor—they'll be wanting to remain in the seat of power. That's why they don't want the borders lowered, trust me."

"Ash has a point," Ruby murmured. "I'd forgotten about the imperial trials. With none of us here to help Tejus, he might not be so successful."

Ash did have a point, but try as I might, I couldn't

forget the genuine underlying fear in the ministers' voices as they'd revealed their inability to lower the borders. I couldn't ignore that. I was also getting a bit annoyed that it seemed like it was Team Ruby and Ash, and neither of them seemed to be considering the possibility that it might all be true.

Jenney had been quiet throughout the exchange, and I turned to her, hoping that she might have some insight.

Jenney shrugged. "I'm sorry, Hazel. I don't know what to think. I've never heard anything about secret stones hidden in the castle, or this entity, and I've lived here all my life—and you wouldn't believe the stuff I've heard that I wasn't meant to."

"It doesn't mean we'll give up," Ruby added. "Maybe we can look into finding our own way through the borders. Maybe Julian was right all along."

"Maybe," I agreed reluctantly.

I wasn't so sure it was just a case of getting through the borders now though…I felt like something big was about to hit Nevertide, and that all of us, Tejus and his ministers included, were ill equipped to deal with it.

"I'm going back upstairs. I just need to fetch something from Benedict's room first," I muttered. Ruby nodded, and concern flittered across her features.

"I'm fine," I said. "I'm just tired. Tired of all of this, actually."

"Me too," she agreed softly.

I left them sitting on the sofas, and made my way to the room that Benedict and Julian had shared. My brother was curled up in the furthest corner of his bed, snoring. I deliberated about whether to wake him or not, but after the day he'd had, I eventually concluded that it was better for him to sleep it off.

I found his clothes, draped over an easy chair, and started to rifle through the pockets of his jeans. I wasn't in the habit of violating my brother's privacy like this, but I figured he'd be fine with it once he heard what the ministers had been saying.

Digging around in the pockets, I came up empty—not so much as an old candy wrapper.

Perhaps he's put it somewhere safe?

I hoped so. It would be better than carrying it around with him. I would ask him in the morning where he'd put it and then deliver the stone to Tejus or put it back where Tejus had thought it was all along—in the crystal room that I'd slept in during my first nights at Hellswan.

I left Benedict's room, shutting the door behind me.

"Did you find what you were looking for?" Ruby asked.

She was waiting for me outside the room. The others had gone.

"No, but it's okay, I'll get it in the morning."

Out of nowhere she enveloped me in a bear-hug. "I'm sorry about tonight. I guess I just find this place so confusing—I don't know what to think anymore. Even stupid things like storms are making me nervous now. There just seems to be so much we don't know."

"It's fine," I replied, my voice muffled by her shirt. "I know exactly how you feel. I'm going to do some digging anyway, see what I find… I'll let you know if anything comes up." I untangled myself from her embrace. I wanted to get to Tejus's quarters to see if he was going to shed any light on the meeting today—if he told me anything at all.

I said my goodbyes to Ruby, and then made my way along the hallways to the other end of the castle and back up the winding staircase. I wondered if Tejus would have come to the same conclusion that Ash had—he'd certainly sounded doubtful in the meeting. I wasn't sure if the idea of everyone ignoring the ministers was a positive thing or not. If there was even a small chance that they were right, then we were all in danger. If this 'entity' was able to control something as powerful as a border surrounding an entire dimension, then who knew what else it was capable of?

Hazel

When I entered my living quarters, I found Tejus sitting on the floor, surrounded by old, large books. There were multiple volumes, most splayed out across the room, open on their spines—some written in runes, with gruesome-looking etchings.

"Where have you been? I told you to stay here," Tejus said as I approached, without looking up from the books.

"I had to see Ash and Ruby. What are you doing?" I asked, swiftly changing the subject and taking out the image Ruby had given me of the rune.

"Will you ever do as you are told?" he grunted at me, then, sighing in frustration, he responded to my question.

"Research. On this castle and the histories of the kingdoms…most of it written by long-winded ministers who died centuries ago."

"Have you come across anything like this?" I asked, showing him the piece of paper.

He took it from me, inspecting it with a furrowed brow.

"No…" he murmured distractedly. "I don't think so. Where did you find it?"

"Ruby and Ash saw it smeared in blood on the wall of a barn – along with a dead goat." I swallowed. Saying it out loud like that didn't feel good.

Tejus nodded slowly.

"Right. I'll see if I can find it. Perhaps in some of the older documents." He studied the paper again, and then placed it on the floor in irritation, rubbing his temples.

I leaned down to pick up a particularly tattered volume. I flicked through some of the pages, sending a plume of dust up into my face. I coughed, and stared down at an image of a sword, with small, cramped notes detailing its design.

"Is this the sword of Hellswan?" I asked, peering at the picture. I thought I recognized the ornate pommel.

Tejus looked back up distractedly and glanced at the open page.

"Yes, it's been around for a while—but the blade keeps getting remade."

I flicked through the pages, but a lot of the text was meaningless to me, either too small to read at a glance, or in letters that didn't make sense. It looked like a history of weaponry, which wasn't of much interest.

I placed the book back on the floor and pretended to look at the other volumes, while watching Tejus out of the corner of my eye. He looked agitated—the more he searched the books and then discarded them, the more frustrated he seemed to get. I wondered if he was looking for the emperor's book, the one that no one else could read. I wondered what that actually meant—and surely only a spell could ensure something like that happened? Unless of course, it was more old sentry magic that I didn't understand… like their True Sight and mind syphoning.

Tejus kept moving his long hair out of his eyes, dragging his hands through it as if he wanted to yank it out in clumps. His jaw was set in a determined, grim line and though he seemed to be barely aware of my presence, I couldn't help but feel a warm, queasy sensation in the pit of my stomach.

My eyes were drawn to his hands as he ran his fingers over the pages. I remembered the pressure of his fingers digging into my back and arms, and the times he'd held me when I'd been afraid... I swallowed.

What did I actually have in common with Tejus? How much did I even know about him other than what he'd told me about himself? And none of that was promising. *I'm more selfish than you could ever imagine,* he'd once said. He was cold, bordering on the heartless, and he had appalling taste in women if Queen Trina was anything to go by. I thought of Wes, the guy I'd met at Murkbeech Summer Camp, before his mind had been messed with by the sentries. He'd been open, warm and kind, and I'd noticed my attraction to *him* right away—the easy smile and welcoming conversation. That was the kind of guy I should have developed a crush on, that could have led somewhere satisfying. Continuing to foster feelings for the stony man sitting next to me only felt like a recipe for pain—more than I'd experienced already.

"If you're going to sit here, you could help," Tejus commented.

"I don't know what you're looking for," I replied evenly.

"Don't you?" He gave me a level look.

"Uh...no, why would I?"

I felt uncomfortable under his gaze, like he could see

right through me.

"Hazel." He smirked. "I know you were listening in on the meeting. I'm not a fool. I know when you're around, and I know your penchant for eavesdropping."

I scowled at him, covering up my embarrassment at being found out.

Hazel, you idiot.

"What do you mean, you know when I'm around?" I asked, wondering if I was on the cusp of learning about yet another sentry ability.

Tejus looked briefly uncomfortable, and cleared his throat.

"Since we mind-melded, our bond has become stronger—I can… sort of sense when you're near."

Oh. That's strange.

"Well," I retorted, trying to ignore the fluttering in my stomach his words caused, "I followed you because I didn't know if you would tell me the truth about what the ministers said. It's in my own interest that these borders come down as soon as possible—it seemed too important an opportunity to miss."

Tejus raised an eyebrow at me, saying nothing. I couldn't believe that he'd known all along—he didn't even seem to be that annoyed about it.

"Hang on," I said, a thought hitting me. "If you knew I was there, why did you say such horrible things about wanting to get me out of the castle—about all of us? Didn't you care how that might make me feel? Especially as I'd only asked a moment before to move out of your quarters—leaving you in peace!"

He looked faintly surprised at my outburst.

"I'm saying those things so that the ministers take the issue seriously. I thought they were just making a power play. I didn't intend for you to take them personally."

"How else was I supposed to take them?"

"Well, I apologize if you did." Tejus had the grace to look at least somewhat apologetic.

I fell quiet, now feeling humiliated. I sounded like a whiny teenager wondering why her crush wasn't all that into her. *Get a grip.*

"So, you're taking what they said seriously?" I asked after a while.

"I'm not sure yet," Tejus muttered. "I'm looking for some proof, trying to find some mention of the entity, one that isn't just hearsay and rumor...I remember vague recollections of being told stories as a young boy, but nothing much, nothing that can really be of any use."

"Okay, I'll help."

I picked up one of the books that stood waiting in a pile, the ones he hadn't gotten to yet. Once again, the pages contained little I understood, but I kept looking through, hoping that something might leap out at me – even if I could find out more information on that ugly rune it would help. Tejus returned to the task too, seeming even more focused than he was before.

"Hazel," Tejus interrupted after a few moments, taking the book out of my hand. "There are lots of things you don't understand about sentries—about Nevertide…about our way of life."

I frowned at him. "Yeah," I replied, gesturing at the books. "Isn't that what we're doing here?"

"No, I mean about us…our…" He paused, swallowing hard. "Our connection. What happened at the night of the coronation."

My stomach clenched in anticipation. His voice was soft and throaty, as if the words were difficult to get out.

"I know you don't…understand why I am the way I am, and I realize that my behavior may seem confusing, but trust me, you should be grateful that I'm willing to set you free. It could so easily not be the case."

He turned away from me, refocusing on the books.

I drew in a breath. Now that he'd broached the subject

of our kiss, albeit vaguely, I dared express what was on my mind. "Tejus… I don't understand. I don't understand what we are… and I don't understand what I am to you."

He continued to page through books, his eyes away from me, though it looked like every muscle in his jaw had tensed. Finally he spoke, his voice surprisingly unsteady.

"I shouldn't have kissed you," he said.

"Then why did you? I still don't understand."

"It's best that you don't," he replied. "And anyway, now… it's not the right time to explain. We need to focus on the entity. I'm concerned for my people, Hazel. I may not believe all that the ministers said, but I can't ignore the fear in their voices."

I nodded, lowering my eyes. Disappointment gripped me, but he was right. As much as I wanted to get some understanding about what was going on between the two of us, I also knew that the borders had to come first—if not for my sake, then for Benedict's, Ruby's and Julian's sakes. If this 'entity' was what was standing in the way of us getting home, then the mystery needed to be solved— and fast.

"Tejus, I've got something to tell you," I murmured, still feeling hesitant about what I was going to reveal. I stood up, moving away from him and toward the window.

I needed to put some space between us if I was to start thinking straight.

I thought about the conversation I'd had with Ruby and Ash and how neither of them had believed me. It looked like my only ally at the moment was Tejus—and he needed all the support that I could give him. It wasn't like the ministers were a lot of help.

He stayed silent while I deliberated. Eventually I turned back round to face him.

"My friends and I, we come from a place called The Shade. When you took us, we were on a camping trip for our summer vacation. The Shade is filled with supernatural creatures. It was originally founded by vampires, but now there are others." I hesitated, finally meeting his shocked gaze.

"And you?" he asked.

"I'm human," I clarified quickly. "So are Benedict and my two friends. But my mother and father are not...nor are my grandparents. It's a long story." I managed a weak smile. "The reason I'm telling you this is that the inhabitants of The Shade—led by my grandfather—have formed something called GASP, which is basically a supernatural protection unit. They help with this sort of thing all the time—dragon issues, rogue vampires, jinn,

Hawks, witches, merfolk, werewolves…you name it, they've done it or *are* it. The members are made up of all sorts of supernatural creatures, and we have allies all over the place, both on Earth and in the supernatural dimension. They could help solve the issue of the entity— I know they could. But we need to get those barriers down."

Tejus was silent for a long moment, staring at me, as if he was seeing me for the first time.

"You're the daughter of vampires?" he asked, wide-eyed.

"Yes."

"I suppose it makes sense, in a way," he murmured after a pause, more to himself than me. "Your mental power— so strong for one so young…and your adaption to all…this." He waved his hands around the room. "Being taken to another dimension, and acting as if it was a mere inconvenience…asking if I was a warlock the day we first spoke."

Oh, yes. I remembered that conversation. It had been the first thing I'd thought on seeing Tejus, after having experienced the sentries' strange mind power.

"Is it not strange being human in a world full of supernaturals?" he asked.

"No. I guess it would be strange to others, but I've

grown up in that world."

He nodded slowly, and I could almost see the million other questions running around his head.

"Does your family still believe you to be at the camp?"

"I have no way of knowing, but they will figure it out sooner or later."

"And then I'll have an entire army of angry supernaturals at my doorstep?" Tejus asked.

"Well, yes." I smiled melancholically, thinking of my parents and the whole GASP crew showing up, meeting Tejus. "But if we get the barriers lowered, I promise you the only thing my parents will get their revenge on will be the entity."

"Well, I am doing everything within my power to remove them," he replied solemnly.

I felt my anxiety ebb at his reassurance, like a weight had lifted from my shoulders, even if only a small one. Some of the tension that had built up between us the last few days also seemed to loosen as we sat together in the span of silence following his assurance. I wondered if it was because I believed that Tejus would keep his word, or if the feeling actually came from being completely honest with Tejus for the first time since we'd met. I hoped that he'd eventually return the favor.

"I was also wondering about the stone," I said, changing the subject. "The one that came from the sword of Hellswan. Do you think that had anything to do with the stones that control the entity?"

"Perhaps," he mused softly. "I believe that it was a stone my father wanted Jenus to have...but we need to know more before we can jump to conclusions. And as powerful as that stone seems to be, I don't believe it alone is going to help us lower the barriers."

I didn't either. If an entire group of ministers couldn't manage it, I doubted the stone alone would be of much help.

"Well," Tejus said, breathing out and leaning back against the base of a chaise longue, "you have given me a great deal to think about, Hazel Achilles."

As he spoke my name and gazed at me with his dark piercing eyes, I felt an urge to be in his arms—for him to hold me in the same way he'd done the other night. I felt closer to him than before. He might still remain a stranger to me for the most part, but I felt that at least he was getting to know *me* a bit better.

A look of warning flashed in his eyes, and I blushed, looking down to the floor.

Ugh.

My intentions must have been written across my face.

"You should get some sleep," he said, clearing his throat. "It's late."

I nodded and hastily rose to my feet. As I moved toward the door, I heard him settle back down on the floor and pick up another heavy volume. Clearly he wouldn't be getting any sleep tonight.

"Oh, Hazel?" He spoke again before I shut the door.

"Yes?" I turned to look at him. Eyes widening, I felt an odd sense of trepidation.

He hesitated before replying.

"Do you… have a betrothed…back in 'The Shade'?"

My jaw dropped. *What?*

"N-No," I managed.

Why would he think that? I'd hardly go around kissing other people if I had.

"I was merely curious," he replied vaguely— infuriatingly vaguely—before his eyes averted once again to the books.

When I finally left him and reached my bedroom, I shut its door behind me, glad to have arrived in relative sanctuary. Leaning against the door, I shook my head.

No human or supernatural had ever confused me as much as Tejus Hellswan.

BENEDICT

The first thing I did when I woke up was look over at Julian's still empty bed. Over the last few days I had hoped that he'd just appear out of nowhere, having taken himself off on some adventure around Nevertide to look for a break in the boundaries. But as the length of his disappearance grew, I couldn't help but experience a gnawing feeling that I was somehow to blame…that I might have unknowingly hurt my friend.

The feeling had increased after seeing the rune on the wall of the barn. I had recognized it instantly. I didn't know how exactly, but the shape felt so familiar, like I knew it as well as my own name…as if it was something that *I* could have drawn.

It had scared me.

I no longer knew what I was capable of doing, and clearly I no longer had any control over my actions when I was asleep. If I'd harmed Julian while I was sleepwalking, then I didn't think I'd ever be able to forgive myself.

I'd made a decision as we left the village yesterday— after the warning from the old man, who had somehow known all about the voices and the rune on the wall—that whether or not Julian's disappearance was my fault, I was going out to search for my friend on my own.

I'd had enough of being in the castle with the voices every night and the stones, and though the forests that lay beyond the village and the meadows were terrifying in their own way, they didn't scare me as much as another night of being possessed by strange voices. Being alone out there didn't scare me either. At least it would mean that I was away from my friends – and that I couldn't harm them.

Queen Trina had told me that the power calling to me was a good one, that it was calling on me to fulfill my destiny. I didn't believe that any more. There was no way that any of this was good—it felt too sick and twisted to be anything but evil. And I no longer wanted to take part in its stupid, dangerous games.

"Benedict?" Yelena appeared at my bedroom door.

It was only just dawn. What was she doing up?

"Yes?" I groaned, wondering what I was going to be nagged about now.

"Can I talk to you a minute?" she asked.

"Um, I was about to go and see my sister," I lied. "Can't it wait?"

"It will only take a second," she persisted, closing the door behind her. She sat down on my bed, her feet tapping agitatedly on the frame.

Please, make yourself at home.

"What is it?" I asked, wanting her to hurry up and get to the point so I could leave.

She eyed my clothing curiously. I was wearing a thick cloak over a thinner, silk one and had belted both securely round my waist.

"You're going to see your sister?" she clarified suspiciously.

"Yes...no—it doesn't matter—what do you want?"

Why did Yelena always have to be so nosy?

She folded her arms grumpily. We stared at one another, waiting to see who would break first. Eventually she sighed, and rolled her eyes.

"Fine. I don't care where you're going. It's where you've *been* that's bothering me."

I was instantly alert. Did Yelena know what had been happening to me during the night? Had she been spying on me?

"What do you mean?" I asked sharply.

"I know you've been sleepwalking. I've watched you leave in the middle of the night, always looking ahead as if you don't even see the room around you." She shuddered. "It's scary. I tried to follow you a couple of times—well, I did follow you a couple of times, but then I'd have to turn back…it would be so cold and dark, but you'd just keep going. Even if I called to you, you would ignore me. I'm worried about you, wandering the castle like that. You're going to get yourself in trouble, eventually. I didn't want to tell on you, like tell Ruby or Hazel or anyone, but you need to stop it. I get worried you're not going to come back each morning, like you might fall off a balcony or down the stairs…" She trailed off, clearly imagining all of the different ways I could meet my end. She didn't know the half of it.

"Well… You should just mind your own business," I said.

Someone—especially Yelena—seeing me in that state,

when I was so…vulnerable, made me mad for some reason.

"I was!" she hissed. "But you kept waking me up—and this castle's creepy enough without one of us taking midnight trips like…like…you're possessed or something!"

Like I'm possessed.

Having Yelena reach the same conclusion I had only half-realized made me feel sick with fear. I sank back down onto my bed, staring at the floor. I felt cold and tired, and utterly sick of whatever was going on here. I wanted it to stop.

"I'm just worried about you," Yelena continued. "You should be worried about you too…I was hoping that maybe I could help."

It was a nice offer, I supposed. But I didn't know how she could. I was just better off getting out of this castle.

"I don't know," I managed eventually. "I don't know how to stop it. There are these voices in my head, driving me forward. I don't know what it is, but it's so powerful, and I can't ignore it."

Yelena blanched.

"What do the voices want you to do?" she whispered.

I swallowed. "Find stuff in the castle. Go to places and pick up these special stones. They glow and *move*—all by themselves. I haven't picked them up yet, but they want me to. And sometimes I wake up outside the castle...that's even scarier. I've tried locking my room, but it doesn't seem to matter. I get out anyway...always ending up somewhere other than my bed...I know I was out last night for instance – because there was mud and sand on my shoes, but I don't remember a thing."

Yelena held her body tighter, staring at me with her huge, blue eyes as large as saucers.

"We need to stop this," she breathed.

"Yeah." I sighed. "Look, I lied to you earlier. I'm going out to try to find Julian in the forest... I was going to stay out, to search until I found him. I kind of felt that it would be better if I stayed away from here, stayed away from my friends...but maybe we can do something? Maybe you could follow me, and tell me in the morning what I've been doing?" I asked hopefully. It would be better than not knowing, and even if I wouldn't be aware of it at night it brought me a bit of comfort to know that while I wandered the castle, at least I wouldn't be alone.

"You shouldn't go into the forest!" Yelena voiced in alarm.

"I have to." I shook my head. "I think that Julian's disappearance might be my doing...somehow. I'm not sure. But I have to try to find him. I have to," I added determinedly.

"It's so dangerous!"

"I know that—but I'm small, I can slip past things if I need to, hide among the trees..." Even as I spoke, I realized how little conviction my voice held. I cleared my throat. "But if I come back tonight, will you watch over me while I sleep?"

She hesitated.

"Don't you think Hazel and Ruby need to know about this?" she asked.

"Eventually yes—but I'll just worry them both sick. Let's wait until we know exactly what's happening, then we can tell them."

She didn't look pleased with the arrangement.

"Please, Yelena. I-I need your help."

"Okay," she replied uncertainly. "I'll do it. Just promise me you'll be careful in the forests. I hear noises coming from them sometimes—horrible noises." She looked out the window, her face still ghost-white with fear.

"Not as bad as the noises in my head," I replied. "Trust me."

She nodded slowly and I exhaled in relief. The whole conversation had given me a bit more hope. Maybe Yelena and I could get to the bottom of this and stop it ourselves without having to bother the others—they had enough on their plate with Julian and the ongoing saga with the barriers.

"Thanks, Yelena, I really appreciate it," I said awkwardly.

She gave me a very small smile.

"Are you going to be less mean to me after this?" she asked.

I blushed.

"Yeah, well, you know…I kind of thought you were a bit out of your depth with all this stuff before—but I was wrong. Sorry," I muttered under my breath while looking at the floor.

"That's a terrible apology."

I shrugged.

"Whatever." She smiled properly this time. "It's all cool. I'll see you later tonight."

"Thanks," I murmured.

"Good luck out there… You'll need it."

RUBY

Ash had asked me to wait for him in the garden that we'd visited together during the trials. It wasn't exactly the perfect day for sitting outside—the sky was still as murky as it had been yesterday, but it was nice to get a second opportunity to be away from the castle, and finally, *finally*, we had some time to ourselves. The guards were continuing their search around Nevertide and we had exhausted ourselves looking in the castle and village. Unless we were willing to brave the forests—something that Ash had put his foot down on—there was nothing else to do but wait to hear from the guards.

I felt apprehensive. Not just about Julian—that was a

constant worry that had sort of lurked at the back of my mind ever since he'd gone missing—but also about spending time with Ash. Being around other people constantly might have been annoying, but it also provided a safety barrier between us, neither of us having to acknowledge what our feelings were toward one another, or talk about what had happened after the disk trial. I still felt a twinge of guilt every time someone brought up the trials, annoyed that I hadn't been able to help him more, that we'd come so far and yet lost at the last hurdle. It was a devastating blow for Ash, and though he tried to put on a brave face most of the time, I could see that it still pained him.

I'd never quite worked out how I'd managed to find myself in the hallway of the castle that night, nor why I'd woken with so little energy. I supposed it didn't really matter now, but occasionally, when I happened to walk past the spot where I'd been found, I felt a sense of unease, like I could half-remember something, but then it would be gone, and I couldn't keep a hold on the memory. I hadn't mentioned it to anyone since the trials, and I didn't want to dwell on it when there was so much going on already...but the thought that I'd been lying, unprotected and unconscious, in the halls of the Hellswan castle in the middle of the night kind of freaked me out.

I smiled as Ash's familiar form approached through a gap in the ivied wall of the garden. I was sitting right at the end of the overgrown pathway, on a small patch of grass beneath what looked like a sycamore tree—the same place where we'd sat the first time we visited. Ash looked up and waved, smiling to himself. In his hand he carried a large wicker basket. It dawned on me what was happening here.

"A picnic?" I asked teasingly.

"You owe me one." He grinned back, plonking himself down on the grass and pushing the basket toward me. Before the trials had truly gotten underway, Ash had asked if I'd wanted to have a picnic with him, and I'd refused—wanting us both to keep our mind on the trials, and not each other. Now there was nothing stopping us…and I guessed this counted as our first actual date.

My face reddened.

"What did you bring?" I asked brightly, turning my attention to the basket. I opened it and found a loaf of bread, juice, fruit, and a bunch of other items all wrapped up in paper and tied with string. Ash—or Jenney—had outdone themselves. It was a feast.

"Everything I could." He smirked. "Are you going to

look at me, Shortie, or just keep rifling through the basket?"

I looked up at him, laughing.

"Sorry," I whispered. "This feels kind of weird."

"I know. It's because we haven't spent any time together," he replied, taking hold of both my hands. His were quite warm, and he stroked the back of my hands gently. Suddenly the gray sky, the picnic and the dampness of the grass ceased to matter. All I was aware of was Ash, his pale face intent on mine, and the broadness of his body that seemed to shelter us both.

"I'm assuming that you don't regret what happened between us?" he asked with a cocky smile. For a moment I wondered how he could be so confident, but then realized that without me noticing, my body had leant toward his, our faces now only inches apart. Evidently, my feelings were obvious.

"No," I replied. "Do you?"

"Absolutely not. I wanted you the moment I saw your angry, dirty face through Jenus' cellar—and I've wanted you more every day ever since."

My stomach flipped, and I found myself struggling to respond.

I didn't need to.

Ash leaned down, closing the inches of space between us. I felt the soft brush of his lips against mine, holding me in a sweet chaste kiss for a moment, before I leaned into him, deepening the pressure—wanting more of his body against mine, and to taste the warmth of his mouth. His arms wrapped around me, pulling me up sideways on to his lap. He ran a hand down my spine, and I gasped into his mouth. Our bodies entwined more closely, so that we almost became one. I never wanted his touches to end, to have to suffer the loss of his mouth melded around mine. My breathing hitched, and our kisses deepened, his hands pushing against me firmly, tracing the outlines of my form, running along my ribcage, and gently brushing against my breasts till I was shivering all over in anticipation.

"We need to stop," he whispered hoarsely against me. "We're outside."

A soft moan escaped from the back of my throat.

"Yeah, I know," I replied reluctantly, recovering and moving back slightly, but still clasped within the cradle of his arms.

"You drive me crazy, Ruby," he murmured into my hair.

The feeling was mutual.

I'd had crushes on other guys my age in The Shade and had kissed a few of them. But none of them had even come close to the effect that Ash had on me. I didn't know whether it was the mind-melding or all that we'd been through together, but I'd never felt so close to another person outside of my friends and family before. Even though there were things that were unsaid between us, and a divide caused by our worlds being so far apart, I felt like Ash saw me differently to the way other people did. Even at my worst, and those days in the cellar had *definitely* been my worst, Ash still wanted me. Still saw the best in me.

"Ash, have you thought about coming back with me, to my world, once the borders are down?" I asked hesitantly.

He looked into my eyes, pushing a lock of hair back behind my ear.

"I have thought about it," he replied slowly.

"And?"

"I don't know. Would *you* want me to come back with you?" he asked.

"I think it could be good. There are lots of jobs where I come from, more alternatives for you than just servant or minister... plus you'd get to watch that TV thing I was telling you about." I smiled teasingly.

He laughed, and kissed my collarbone. It sent another

round of shivers cascading through my body.

"That doesn't really answer my question," he replied.

"I want you there."

As soon as the words left my mouth, I knew they were true. I did want Ash to come back with me when we returned to Earth. He might have been born in Nevertide, but Ash was more human than a lot of humans I'd met. He deserved the chance at a life outside of this dimension—and I wanted to be with him when it unfolded.

"Am I interrupting something?"

I jerked away from Ash at the sound of an invasive, feminine voice splintering through the peace of the garden.

Queen Trina Seraq stood a few yards from us, looking imperious in her royal blue robes, and covered in glittering jewels. Ash and I hastily untangled ourselves from one another.

"Your Highness," Ash acknowledged.

She smiled down at him, nodding her head gracefully. As Ash moved to get to his feet, she turned to stare at me, her eyes cold, but the smile remaining fixed in place.

"Ruby, a pleasure to see you again... though I would have thought you'd have left by now?"

I hesitated, wondering how much I was meant to divulge about the borders, but it seemed strange that Queen Trina wouldn't know about them.

"The borders remain," Ash replied, taking the onus off me.

Queen Trina laughed. "Oh, how silly of me. Of *course*. Such a mystery…the Hellswan ministers are so cloak and dagger, aren't they?"

I returned her smile weakly. I didn't believe for a second that she'd 'forgotten' that the Nevertide borders hadn't yet come down—so what had been the point in that brief charade?

"Ashbik," she continued, moving swiftly on from the subject, "I have a proposition to make to you. I was so impressed with your performance in the trials—genuinely, truly impressed with someone so young and of *undistinguished* birth having such abilities—that I wanted to offer you the position of royal advisor in my kingdom."

I gaped at her.

That was a double-edged compliment if ever I heard one.

What a cow!

Ash stood silent for a moment. I looked up at him, trying to read his expression, but it was impassive. I felt relieved that he wasn't jumping at the offer.

"I could use a man like you," she continued. "I don't want the Hellswans getting another chance at Nevertide rule—the imperial trials will start soon. Assist me, and it's your chance to make a real difference in all the kingdoms, not just your own."

"It's a generous offer," Ash acknowledged.

"It is," retorted the queen, her eyes flashing. "And it won't be on the table forever."

"Understood. I would like some time to think it over."

Queen Trina's glare then shot to me, as if I was the reason for his hesitation. I kept my expression impassive— I wasn't going to be intimidated by her. She wasn't *my* queen, and though she'd been helpful to Ash in the trials, I didn't feel that either of us owed her anything. Abelle's warning rang in my ears.

"You have till tomorrow. Then the offer is off the table." She spun around, heading in the direction of the garden's entrance. "Oh, one thing." She flashed a smile. "You might also think about getting your humans home, Ash—it doesn't look like the Hellswan ministers are capable of doing what needs to be done. If those borders were to remain in the power of the Hellswans…well, you might never lift them." She shrugged, her eyes gleaming, and then turned to leave us.

"What do you think?" Ash turned to me as soon as she'd left, his eyes bright.

"I don't know… I'm not sure how much I trust her…" I hedged, not wanting to cast a complete downer on the offer without knowing how Ash felt first.

Ash turned to look in the direction she'd just exited.

"I agree," he said eventually. "But I don't know if I trust Tejus any more than I do her. Or the Hellswan ministers."

I nodded. We agreed on that point, at least…but still, there was something about Queen Trina that unnerved me, that I couldn't quite place a finger on. It could have just been Abelle's warning, and that I'd been swayed by her concern, but I thought she was right to be wary of the woman. And I'd promised that I'd look out for Ash.

"I get that, but I just wonder if she's got…other motives," I finished lamely.

"Everyone's always got other motives," Ash reasoned. "But that doesn't mean I can't take advantage of the offer. It would be a big step up for me. And she's right—I don't want the position of emperor going to a Hellswan. I could help make a real difference – you need to understand; the whole of Nevertide has been suffering for a while. We've been having near constant bad crop yields. Nothing seems to be growing anymore. Taxes are astronomical, and no one can keep up. Sentries all over Nevertide have it bad, not just in Hellswan ."

"I do understand that, but what about *you*, Ash? What about what we were just talking about—you leaving Nevertide?" I asked softly, feeling like I was out in the cold a bit and not really part of Ash's decision-making process. I knew I had no right to be, really, it was his life, but I'd thought a moment ago he'd seemed keen to return to my dimension.

"It would be until then," he replied hurriedly. "Unfortunately I'm not holding out much hope for the borders anytime soon, what with Tejus left in control."

Okay. Not what I wanted to hear.

"We don't know that for sure. Hazel's doing everything she can," I retorted.

He came and sat back down next to me.

"I'm sorry," he replied more gently. "I know. I just think that this could be a good opportunity. Like you and Hazel in the trials, spreading your bets so that you had a better chance of returning home. If we align with the queen for a short while, it might help you in the long run."

His 'you' didn't escape my notice. Had he changed his mind so quickly? I didn't want to believe that. Ash was impulsive, but this impulsive? I preferred instead to put it down to the initial excitement of the job offer. Maybe when he had more time to think, he would consider his options more carefully.

"And I guess you would stay in Queen Trina's kingdom?" I asked, suddenly realizing that we might be separated. I didn't know if I could bear Hellswan castle without Ash.

"I was hoping…that if I took the job, you would come with me?"

"I can't leave my friends, Ash," I said quietly.

There was no way I could abandon them—not while Julian was still missing, which also left Benedict without any of us around while Hazel remained with Tejus in his quarters.

"I understand," he sighed. "I suppose I need to know more. Maybe I could have another talk with Queen Trina, work out the details before I make my decision."

"That sounds like a good idea," I replied slowly.

Selfishly, I wanted him to refuse the position outright.

"Aren't you offended by what she said about your birth?" I asked.

Ash smiled wryly. "That's royalty for you, Shortie. They're all like that—if I want to better myself at all in this world, then I need to get used to it."

"It's not like that in my world," I replied. "You wouldn't have to ever get used to it there."

"But I'd have to get used to a whole load else." He laughed, leaning back against the tree. He pulled me back with him, resting my head against his chest. I listened to the regularity of his heartbeat, knowing that the conversation was over—for now.

Don't go, Ash, I pleaded. *Please don't go.*

Hazel

I'd stopped to look in the human quarters this morning, to see if I could find Benedict to relieve him of the stone, but he wasn't there, and none of the kids had seen him. Ash and Ruby were also absent – Jenney murmured something about Ash looking into new job offers – so I hoped he was with them. Not sure what else to do, I left a note in his room telling him to come and find me as soon as he was in, then I rejoined Tejus to continue going through the old volumes of the ministers, hoping that we could find mention of the 'entity' that was currently holding Nevertide on lockdown.

"We're going to go to the castle library," Tejus told me

as soon as I ascended the winding staircase to his rooms.

We went back the way I'd come and crossed the main belly of the castle into another wing.

"This was Danto's favorite place. I never visited it much," Tejus commented as he wrenched open the cobwebbed door to the room. Clearly no one had been here in a while. It was no wonder the ministers didn't know a thing, if no one was willing to take an interest in the history of their land.

Tejus held the door open for me, and I stepped into a huge room. Here, the gray stone of the rest of the castle had been partly replaced with red-veined marble. The room was divided by huge arches, and books lined every available surface. To the left of the entrance, there was a stained-glass window, reaching upward to the eaves of the ceiling. A reading table was positioned beneath it, with unlit chandeliers running along its length. I wished I'd known about this place earlier—it would have been one of the places in Hellswan castle that I would have enjoyed spending time in.

"Wow," I breathed.

"It's nice, isn't it?" Tejus looked around with disinterest. "Though I'm not entirely sure where we start looking."

"In the history section," I replied.

Tejus glanced at me with a questioning expression. "What do you mean?"

"A history—or nonfiction—section. You must have one?" I repeated slowly, wondering why Tejus was choosing to be so dense.

"Hazel, this is all history. We don't keep 'fiction' here. Made-up stories are for children."

I burst out laughing, mainly because I thought I might cry otherwise—I'd never heard anything so tragic.

"Really, you don't read fiction? No thrillers, mysteries, horror, romances?"

"As children, yes," Tejus repeated tersely. "Do *you* like reading...that sort of thing?"

"Well, yes. It's everything to me...Do other people in Nevertide read fiction? Or is it just royalty who don't?" I asked with genuine curiosity.

"Nobody reads fiction here, Hazel. It distracts from work, and true knowledge."

"Hm. True knowledge?" I countered acerbically. "Well, none of you seem to know all that much."

"Which is why we're here," he snapped. "Follow me."

Tejus led me down rows of books, till we were at the far end of the room. The light here wasn't as good—and the books were even more musty and aged than the rest of the collection. They must have been centuries old. I eyed them with reverence.

Tejus reached for a hefty tome, and leafed through it. "Here, start with this." He heaved the book into my outstretched arms and then loaded me up with a few more. I staggered forward, and he caught my shoulder and pushed me gently upright.

"Be careful—those books are thousands of years old," he chided.

"Thanks," I replied sarcastically.

We took our loads back to the reading table, and Tejus set about lighting the candles. A few moments later the library was cast in a cozy glow, and I smiled at Tejus.

"How can you not like it in here? It's so amazing." I sighed. "There's something really romantic about being surrounded by thousands of books...all those words, and the *smell*—that's what I think I love the most."

Tejus looked at me with barely concealed amusement.

"If I'd known it would make you this happy, I would have taken you here a long time ago," he mused.

"Well, now you know," I replied.

He nodded, and our eyes met briefly across the table. The moment passed, and I returned to the task at hand, flicking through the pages trying to find anything relating to the castle or the entity.

Hours passed, and the wicks of the candles burnt steadily lower. I tried to focus all my attention on the words in front of me, but every so often I could feel Tejus staring at me, and the skin on the back of my neck would flush. But whenever I looked up, he would look away, never meeting my glance.

Soon I could hear raindrops hitting the stained-glass windows in a slow pitter-patter. Before long it was a full-on downpour, and the room seemed to grow even cozier. Looking over at the window, I smiled.

"Look. The stained glass is making the rain look red."

Tejus followed my gaze. He didn't smile. Instead he looked perturbed, and swiftly rose up and out of his chair. Fiddling in frustration with an old latch, he finally managed to push open part of the window.

"It's not the glass. The rain *is* red."

I rose hastily, joining him at the window. We looked upward at the sky. It was cast in dark thunderclouds, the same as it had been for days—but the courtyard below, and the roads surrounding it, were all soaked in blood-red water. I moved to reach my arm out of the window, but Tejus snatched it back.

"Don't," he commanded. "We don't know what it is."

He left me standing at the window, rushing back to the books.

"What?" I asked.

"I think I read something…" he muttered, flicking back through the book he'd been reading.

I waited impatiently for him to find what he was looking for, turning my attention back to the rain. Perhaps it was pollution—I was sure in some parts of the world they got red rain on account of desert dust getting carried into the atmosphere. Though I wasn't entirely sure in those cases if the rain was actually this *red*…It looked like the sky had been sliced open, and was bleeding profusely onto the earth. I shuddered, recalling a story my Uncle Benjamin had once told me. When he and River had been on a boat, travelling from Egypt to The Shade, they'd experienced a bout of red rain. In their case, it had been literal blood—a trick of the jinni, Queen Nuriya. I could only wonder what was behind this phenomenon…

"Here," Tejus muttered, lifting the book up closer to the light. "'If it shall come to pass that the seal is undone by its guardians, the land shall be visited by evils such as the spirit chose, the first of which will be the blood rains, the second the fires of ice, the third will be pestilence of silence,'" he read.

I swallowed. That didn't sound good.

"Do they mention *what* spirit? Is it the entity?" I asked.

Tejus shook his head. "No...I think this is something different...another spirit that helped lock up the entity in the first place. Here, look." He placed the book down on the table, and I started to read.

Most of the volume went into intricate detail on the history of the ministers—who rose to which position and when, who held the greatest sway over the emperor—and, on some of the more tedious pages, how many animals each minister owned on their land. I flicked through quickly, trying to find more information than the paragraph Tejus had found.

Finally, I found another short section that mentioned the entity.

"'And the benevolent power was corrupted, and the great Emperor Thelus had no choice but to bind him from doing further harm, configuring the Hallowed Stones of the Entity to create its own bonds. Thelus and the spirit decree their position as its guardians, so long as this earth shall stand.'"

"Emperor Thelus was from the Seraq kingdom," Tejus said. "This would have been written centuries ago."

I flipped to the front of the book, but there was no date given. I returned to the page I'd just read, scanning forward to see if there was any information on where these 'bonds' actually were, or more detail on the 'spirit'.

"There are a few mentions of the 'Acolytes'," I murmured.

"That was the old cult I told you about. What does it say?" Tejus asked quickly.

"Not much… just that 'a representative of the Acolytes appeared at the council,' but it doesn't say any more. Then they're mentioned again in council attendant lists. It's not much to go on."

I thought of the eerie temple that Tejus and I had found near the Viking remains. Tejus had told me that it belonged to the old cult, but that they hadn't been active in years. I wasn't so sure. That temple looked like someone had been visiting it…

"What if they're responsible for the entity being able to manipulate the barriers? It would only be able to do that if someone broke the seal, right? What if one of them did it?" I asked.

"Like I told you, they're old history. The cult no longer exists, it hasn't for years. They were abolished about two centuries ago."

"How were they abolished?" I asked.

"They were forbidden to practice. Anyone who attended their rituals was sentenced to death."

I raised an eyebrow at him. "And there's no chance they would have carried on in private…or started up again when the threat toward them subsided?"

It didn't sound that likely to me that a mere threat of death would cause the cult to disband. Most cults I'd ever read about never stopped because someone told them to—they were fanatical believers, following their leader or cause with a blind faith impervious to reason.

"I don't think they're our biggest problem right now. Even in the unlikely event that they had restarted their practices, they only ever caused small local issues—ritual sacrifice of farmyard animals and, in rare cases, peasant sentries."

"That's reassuring," I murmured. "Like a dead goat in a barn?"

"Perhaps," Tejus agreed. "Even so – a few fanatics wouldn't have the ability to create a barrier this strong…or this," he gestured to the windows. "Our focus needs to be on locating the stones, searching every inch of the castle if we must…I was thinking of what you said about the sword stone." Tejus started pacing up and down. "Perhaps it *was* part of the seal…I didn't want to believe that my father would be so wholly irresponsible, but if he was desperate enough for Jenus to win the trials…" His voice trailed off.

"He might have thought he had time to put it back, but then he got sick?" I suggested, more to make Tejus feel better than anything else. Anyone who put their sons through the hell of the labyrinth just so he could decide who would be best to represent their house in the trials was not the kind of person I considered responsible. I thought it was highly likely that the king had been that stupid.

Tejus turned to me. "We should fetch the stone."

"Yeah…about that…"

Crap.

HAZEL

Tejus glared at me, furious.

"We need to find Benedict, *now*."

He could barely contain his fury, his jaw flicking with the effort of holding back a tirade that would be directed at me.

"I know," I replied with a gulp. "I only did it because Julian and Ruby found out about the stone…and I thought if Ash knew, you'd be disqualified from the trials."

Tejus closed his eyes and sucked in air sharply through his nose. "Please, Hazel. Spare me your excuses."

I nodded.

"Where is Benedict now?" he asked.

This was getting worse and worse.

"Well—I went to look for him this morning, but he wasn't there. So I'm not sure," I replied quietly. I waited for his explosion, but none came.

"Right. We need to get to the human quarters." Tejus moved swiftly toward the door, expecting me to follow him. I practically tripped over myself trying to keep up with him. The door to the library swung in my face and Tejus marched down the hallway.

As we navigated the castle, ministers kept rushing about, whispering to one another. As soon as they caught sight of Tejus, they tried to approach him, but their sentences were left hanging in mid-air as he marched past them.

I'd never seen the castle this busy except on trial days, and I wondered if it was the red rain that was causing such mayhem.

As I half-ran along behind Tejus, I berated myself again for leaving the stone with my brother. It was all well and good, me pointing the finger at the emperor for being irresponsible, but what about *my* actions? Leaving a potentially devastating weapon in the hands of my brother without even realizing the true extent of its power...I should have known better.

Tejus arrived at the entrance to the human quarters, and I caught up with him as he banged on the door. The guards usually posted there were absent, and my stomach gave a sickening lurch.

The door was opened by Yelena, who jumped back the moment she saw Tejus's menacing frame in the doorway.

"Yelena," I burst out before Tejus had a chance to scare the rest of the humans gathered in the room, "have you seen Benedict?"

She looked around shiftily, avoiding my gaze.

"Um…no."

"Ruby or Ash?" I probed.

"No, I haven't seen them today," she replied with more certainty.

"Yelena, I really need you to tell me if you know where Benedict is, it's really important. He could be in danger."

As soon as the words left my mouth, the truth of them hit me and I wanted to scream. I had put my brother in danger. I would never forgive myself.

She hesitated for a few moments, her blue eyes looking desperate.

"Yelena…" I warned.

"He went out to look for Julian," she whispered.

What?

"He's coming back tonight, he promised he would!" cried Yelena, turning toward the red-soaked window, her face taut and anguished.

"Why would he think that was a good idea?" I yelled out.

"I...I don't know. He didn't want to be in the castle—he just wanted to find Julian," Yelena stuttered.

I groaned.

What have I done?

"Do you know where he went?" I asked Yelena, trying to keep my voice as calm as I could. It wasn't her fault this was happening.

"I think to the forest?" she replied, cringing.

I spun round to face Tejus and started to march back out into the hallway.

"We need to find him."

Tejus grabbed my arm, pulling me back toward him.

"It's almost dark, Hazel—we're better off waiting till he returns."

"What are you talking about?" I gaped at him, not understanding his hesitation. "Of course we can't wait. We have to go, *now*. He'll be alone out there!"

"Which was *his* choice," Tejus emphasized. "He wouldn't have gotten very far. With this rain he's probably just found a barn to hole up in for a while."

"If he hasn't gone far, then we'll find him faster. Let's go!" I pulled my arm out of Tejus's grip, continuing to walk along the hallway.

"Hazel!" Tejus strode to catch up with me. "This is madness—why can't you just wait?"

"Because it's my brother!" I yelled back. I was about to add, "How would you like it?" but then realized who I was talking to—Tejus and his brothers had the most un-brotherly relationship of anyone I'd ever come across.

"I forbid it!" Tejus stopped and stood in front of me, blocking my path.

"You *can't* forbid it—I'm going!" I retorted furiously.

I side-stepped him and broke into a sprint. Tejus caught up with me easily, but it didn't matter—over my dead body would he stop me leaving the castle.

"Hazel, will you please think about this rationally?" Tejus implored.

"Nope." I ignored him, running toward the entrance.

"Fine!" Tejus barked out.

I stopped running and caught my breath.

"If you're going to insist on going anyway, I'm coming with you. We'll head to the stables first—it will be quicker on horseback, it's too dark to see with a vulture."

"Thank you," I replied stiffly.

"This way." He jerked his head toward a smaller hallway off the main entrance, and we hurried down it. We cut through a narrow corridor that was damp and musty, indicating that this was the servants' entrance to the stables. Soon we came to a small door, and Tejus pulled it open.

The stables lay about a yard ahead. Tejus held me back, stopping me from crossing the courtyard. He held out his arm, pulling his robe back so that his skin was exposed to the rain. Without much light, the red drops looked like a sickly tar on his skin, thicker than any rain I'd ever seen. He waited a moment, and then withdrew his arm.

"It's fine. Let's go."

We crossed the courtyard quickly, trying to avoid the worst of the red rain, but it streamed down the back of my neck all the same. I hated the thought of Benedict being stuck out in this. He must have been so afraid.

Tejus yanked the doors to the barn open, and his bull-horse whickered at the presence of its master. He strode toward the stable doors while I waited at the entrance, impatient to get going.

Tejus walked the bull-horse forward. Without speaking to me, he slid his hands around my hips and lifted me with alarming speed up onto the saddle. A second later he jumped on behind me, wrapping his arms around my waist. Moving the horse forward, he grabbed a blanket off a hook by the door and wrapped that round me too, covering the back of my neck and hands.

"Thank you," I muttered.

We cantered across the courtyard, and Tejus bellowed at the guards sheltered under the entrance doors of the castle to raise the portcullis. They rushed forward, cranking it open as we approached. Tejus gave the bull-horse a swift thwack to its hindquarters and it galloped forward, crossing the bridge.

As soon as we reached the raised portcullis, the bull-horse reared up, screaming. I shifted backward, taken by surprise, but Tejus kept his grip tight around me. He urged the horse on, but it would go no further.

Tejus muttered an expletive under his breath.

"Wait here," he instructed, and jumped to the ground. He took a few steps forward, till he was directly under the yawning iron spikes of the portcullis. Then he stopped. I watched as he raised his arms, looking as if he was pushing against an invisible barrier…

"What the HELL is going on?" he roared.

The guards rushed in from behind, waiting to do his

bidding, looking at one another in confusion.

"There's a barrier up!" he yelled over the rain. "Is this the ministers' doing?"

The guards shook their head, but more in confusion than anything else.

"Get me Commander Varga!" he ordered.

"He's still out, looking for Julian the human boy," one of them replied hastily.

Tejus released a roar of frustration.

I got down from the bull-horse, slowly. While Tejus raged at the guards, I approached the gateway. Pushing my hands out, I felt a smooth, supple surface meet my fingers. A barrier. We had been shut in.

"Tejus?" I cried out hoarsely.

He was by my side in seconds.

"Hazel, you need to get indoors. Get out of the rain."

"What is this?" I asked, my voice trembling.

"I don't know yet," he replied. "I'm going to find out... We'll fix this."

"Benedict's still out there."

"I know," he stated curtly, but he wrapped the blanket tighter round my shoulders. He lifted my chin up, so my eyes met his. His face was soaked in red rain; he looked deadly, and desperate.

"Get indoors, Hazel. There's nothing you can do right now. I'll meet you in the room. Go."

The doors to the castle were flung open. In the bright lights of the torches, a storm of ministers appeared on the front steps, all running toward the barrier.

"Go!" Tejus ordered.

Taking a deep breath, I turned and fled.

RUBY

At dawn this morning, Ash had knocked on my door. For a moment I had hoped that he was coming to tell me that he'd changed his mind—that he wouldn't be giving Queen Trina's position any more consideration. But he had smiled broadly at me, and held out a traveling cloak. We were going to take a short trip to her kingdom.

The journey had taken all morning, and now I was sitting in the lavish opulence of Queen Trina's waiting room while Ash had a private meeting with her royal highness. The moment Queen Trina laid eyes on Ash she had smiled with child-like delight. When her gaze had shifted to me, I saw nothing but a satisfied malice in her expression.

I hadn't seen another soul since we entered the castle, but by the looks of the lavish grounds and well-kept interior, Queen Trina employed an entire army of staff...but where were they? It was unnerving, even in the bright light of the afternoon. The heavy storm clouds that had rolled over Nevertide had vanished as soon as we arrived at the palace, but looking back to Hellswan, I could see they hung low and moody everywhere else.

As I waited, I tried to quell some of my misgivings about Queen Trina. If Ash was going to take the job, then I'd better start learning how to keep my mind open. Her support in the trials I could understand—she was clearly making a power play against Tejus, and I didn't hold that against her; no doubt every other ruler in the six kingdoms of Nevertide wanted to do the same. What unnerved me was the way she latched onto Ash. He had performed well in the trials, but I wondered if her interest was more underhanded than that. She would have realized that Ash knew the Hellswan castle better than anyone else, had knowledge of its inhabitants that would no doubt benefit her. But I knew Ash. He wouldn't play dirty—he had already paid the price of doing that with the death of the emperor. But if he refused Queen Trina, would he have to pay an even greater price?

As I contemplated what the queen's strategy might be, a figure approached. As it came closer, I recognized the tell-tale signs of a nymph. What was a nymph doing in Queen Trina's castle?

Before I could ask, the figure hurtled past me, winking, then breaking into peals of giggles. She darted off out of sight, and I leapt to my feet – determined to follow her and get to the bottom of why Queen Trina kept such creatures in her palace. Her faint glow gave her away, leaving a sort of trail that I could follow around the winding pathways of the palace.

Eventually the tracks of the glow faded altogether, and I was standing in front of a large set of doors, with small stools placed either side of it. Sentries sat about, all peasants from the village, and all silent, as if they were in a doctor's waiting room.

The nymph appeared as if from nowhere and opened the door. I called out a, "Hey!" but she slammed the door in my face. The sentries looked at me with interest as I pursed my lips at the nymph's rudeness, but they didn't say anything.

"Are you all here to see the queen?" I asked the general gathering politely.

Some of them ignored me completely, but a few of them nodded.

"We probably won't see her though—more likely her hapless ministers," a bitter voice spat. It belonged to an old man. He was staring at the wall, not looking at me. Next to him was a woman, crying into her shawl.

I walked over to her.

"Are you okay?" I asked.

She looked up, and hastily wiped away her tears.

"It's my feather bleaters," she sniffed. "They died in the night, throats cut, left in a pile in the corner of the pen. They're my livelihood! I don't know who would have done something as cruel as that."

I thought immediately of the goat and the small boy. "Were there any…signs, that you saw?"

"Signs?" she asked, surprised.

"By the…feather bleaters? Like a rune sort of sign?" I clarified.

She shook her head.

"No, I didn't see anything like that."

That was good. Perhaps I'd been right in my initial assumption about the rune—that it was just a form of vandalism by bored sentry teens. Spiteful and cruel, but just kids playing around, not a sign of more violence to come.

The door creaked open, and the nymph popped her head around the door and called a name out, shutting it quickly before I could rise to my feet.

"That's me," muttered the woman as she stood, gathering her voluminous shawls about her and scurrying off toward the door. It opened slightly to admit her, and then was closed once more.

I looked around at the rest of the waiting sentries. None of them made eye contact with me, and I got the impression that conversation would not be welcomed. I leaned back against the wall, determined to wait for the woman to return. If she was satisfied with the outcome, then I would stop snooping around and leave the matter. Perhaps it was totally normal for royalty to keep nymphs in their castles—perhaps they were just playthings here – kept for some weird kind of amusement… I would ask Ash as soon as he was finished with Queen Trina.

I didn't have long to wait.

The door opened again, and the woman stepped out into the hallway. Another name was called, but I rose to speak to the woman before she departed.

"How did it go?" I asked.

"What?" She smiled sleepily at me. Her gray hair, which

had been tied up in a rather severe bun when she entered, was now loose, and it fell in disarray about her shoulders.

"The...feather bleaters, did the matter get solved?" I asked again.

"Oh, yes," she replied. "I must attend to them—they'll be hungry."

"But they're *dead*."

She laughed gaily at my comment. "Don't be silly." She smiled again and tapped my arm. "You're a pretty young thing, go off and play in the meadows."

With that she walked off, weaving from side to side as if she couldn't manage to walk in a straight line. I knew the after-effects of a nymph when I saw them—that woman had been completely stunned.

I sat back down on the stool, waiting to see what would happen when the next sentry left the room. Like the last, this sentry's time with the 'council' didn't last long either—and he came back out with a very self-satisfied look on his face, with half of his shirt torn.

When the next villager's name was called, I tried to beat them to the door. When it opened, I slipped in, forcing my way past the giggling nymph. In an instant, two guards seized me and escorted me back outside, roughly shoving me back on the stool.

"Wait your turn," one of them growled at me.

I hadn't seen much in the room, just that it was large, and all that it had contained was a small table and two chairs either side…hardly evidence of any wrongdoing, and certainly not the pleasure playground I'd half been expecting, but still I felt something was off. Those sentries had definitely been under the influence of nymphs. Was Queen Trina using their magic to meddle with the villagers' grasp on reality or even their memories? And for what purpose? Was it just to make her kingdom run more smoothly, with minimal effort from her? Surely they'd realize what happened when they returned home and would return the next day. It didn't exactly make anyone's life any easier.

I sighed. So much for keeping an open mind about Queen Trina. I now had more misgivings about her than when we'd arrived.

As I made my way back to her office, getting lost a couple of times on the way, I prayed once again that Ash would have changed his mind.

I had only just sat back down on the chaise longue where I'd been told to wait when Ash exited the office, a broad smile across his face.

Damn.

"How did it go?" I asked, forcing a smile.

He waited till the door had been shut behind him and then turned to me, his eyes alight. "Very well. She wants me to join her council, to assist in the imperial trial strategy, and then once that's over have a top position within her council—and that's whether we win or not...but I'm one hundred percent sure we will. Trina was going over the other contestants, they've all got weaknesses we can exploit."

Oh, so it's 'Trina' now, is it?

"Ash, don't you think this is moving a bit fast?" I asked hesitantly, knowing that I was about to burst his bubble— but for his sake, and the unease I felt around the queen, I was unable to hold back.

"Yeah." He shrugged. "But she didn't give me any choice. You know that."

"I know, I just..." I trailed off as he winced.

"Come on, Shortie." He took hold of my hands, wrapping them around his waist as he drew me toward him. "This is a good opportunity for me. I've always wanted to make a difference in the way Nevertide's been run—and now's my chance."

He looked into my eyes—his beseeching, wanting for me to agree with him, to celebrate. But I couldn't. I felt horrible, but Abelle's warning rang in my ears, and no matter how much Ash might resent my behavior, I just couldn't get on board with this.

"Look, there's something I need to tell you." I spoke in a hushed voice, drawing him out into a large open-air courtyard where we'd be less likely to be overheard. I told him what I'd seen that afternoon—the nymphs and the befuddled villagers, and what I thought was going on.

"That's quite an accusation, Shortie," he replied, scratching his head.

"I know," I replied.

"Hm… Let's take a look together. Can you remember the way to the room?"

I nodded, and, looking around to make sure we weren't being followed, I dragged Ash off toward the waiting room.

When we arrived, all the stools were empty. I looked around, confused about how they'd gotten through so many visitors in such a short time.

"They—they were all here," I stammered.

Ash looked around. "I guess they've all gone home."

In frustration I marched up to the doors and yanked one of them toward me. It swung open easily. There were no guards or nymphs anywhere to be seen, just a sentry minister sitting at the desk I'd seen earlier, scribbling away on parchment.

"Um…" I cleared my throat. "Hi, I thought I saw a girl in here earlier, in fact I *know* I saw one… very pretty, covered in leaves…Where is she?"

The sentry lowered his pen and peered at me through half-moon spectacles. "I'm afraid I don't know what you're referring to," he replied. "There's been no one fitting that description here today I'm afraid. Perhaps your imagination is playing tricks on you?" He smirked.

"But I *know* I saw her!" I protested.

Ash placed a hand on my shoulder.

"We're sorry to have disturbed you," Ash replied tightly.

"Ah!" The minister smiled warmly. "Not at all, Ashbik! I hear you are soon to join our little team—you are a most needed and wanted addition, let me assure you."

"That's very kind of you," Ash replied, edging me out of the door. "We'll leave you in peace."

He shut the door behind him, and turned to me, his face marked with disappointment. It was horrible to see— he'd never looked at me like that before, not even when we lost the trials.

"Ash—" I began, but he shook his head.

"I believe you, I do. But we don't know anything more than the fact that you saw nymphs in the palace. There could be a million reasons why they might be here… I think this is more about me moving here not being what you want," he told me. "But it's the way things have to be, for now. Not forever. Let's just see how things go, all right? I promise I won't lose sight of who I am…and if Queen Trina does have any wicked vices, I'll stay clear of them. Deal?" He winked at me, and the tension that had been building all afternoon eased within me. It was Ash—I should have more faith in him. I should trust him to be smart about this, to not be led astray.

"Let's get you home," he sighed, enveloping me in a bear hug.

He lifted me up, and I pressed my cheek against the bare skin of his neck, inhaling the familiar smell of him.

He was right. This wasn't ideal, and I didn't think that I'd ever be in full support of Ash working for Queen Trina…but perhaps things wouldn't be as bad as I feared.

BENEDICT

I was lost.

It shouldn't have come as any surprise. The decision to hike through the forest looking for Julian had been a desperate one—I'd known that before I left, but at the time, anything had seemed better than staying in that castle.

As soon as the main path had become nothing but muddy track, I'd been unable to see what direction I was heading in, and there had been nothing to guide me, just constant clouds hanging overhead.

Then the red rains had started. At first I'd thought I was bleeding, that I'd gashed my head or something in one of my many battles with thorns and brambles, but soon everything was coated in the gross liquid. It mixed with the mud, and I felt it sloshing into my shoes.

But the weather was the least of my worries. The deeper I ventured into the forest, the more clearly the howls of unknown creatures cut through the silence. Sometimes they seemed to get nearer, and sometimes they would be miles away. The noises they made sounded feverish and excited...like they could *smell* me, and were just waiting till I approached near enough to make me their dinner.

I paused every few minutes, making sure that there was no other sound than my own feet—that I wasn't being stalked by some unknown predator. So far I'd been lucky, but that didn't make me feel all that much better. Ever since I'd entered the forest, I'd felt like I was being watched. The hairs on the back of my neck would prickle, and I would spin around, only to be faced with darkness and shadows and misshapen tree trunks.

I would have given anything to come to a landmark—a break in the forest, a hut of some kind that I could run inside and lock the door against whatever creatures lurked out here in the open. I knew Julian wasn't around here anywhere. There was no way that anyone in their right mind would stay out here... no matter how desperate they were to get away from the castle.

Another howl tore through the air. In fright, I stumbled, and landed flat on the ground. It hurt like hell, but I lay there a few moments, waiting to hear if the wolf, or whatever it was, would make another noise, so I'd know if it was approaching me or moving away.

Please, I prayed, *please don't let me die like this.*

The howl sounded again. I breathed a sigh of relief. It had moved away. Hastily I scrambled to my feet, noticing for the first time that it wasn't mud that I'd landed on, but sand. I paused, trying to listen. What I'd assumed was leaves rustling in the trees for the last few miles was actually the sound of the sea.

I scrambled forward. The ground was becoming rockier now, and as I moved ahead, I noticed the trees were becoming less dense. I was leaving the forest behind! I was pretty sure that it would be better to spend the night in a cave by the coast than spend another minute surrounded by the trees. As I moved forward as quickly as I could, I recalled my promise to Yelena—that I would return to the castle tonight. I felt a pang of guilt. She would be really worried, and I had made her swear not to tell anyone. Still, it was Yelena, I figured she'd definitely tell.

Climbing over a large rock, I dropped to the ground.

No!

As I looked around me, I saw the eerie green light ahead of the Viking graveyard.

No...not this place!

I'd arrived in the last place in the world that I wanted to be. The forest would be better than this. I turned back toward the rock, trying to ignore the green light. It was already beckoning me forward. My fingers dug into the rough surface of the stone; I was determined not to turn around. Determined not to have my will taken from me again.

Benedict...

The whispers had started.

"No!" I hissed into the night. "I'm not doing this anymore! I don't want to! Just leave me ALONE!"

This is the way home, Benedict...

I shook my head, clinging to the rock with every ounce of energy within me.

Don't you want to go home? They're waiting for you...

The pull became stronger. I started to sob as my hands relaxed of their own accord, lying gently on the rock. My shoulders dropped, and I turned around slowly toward the green light. I had lost.

I made my way down into the temple, running my

fingers along the brightly glowing runes—remembering them, feeling like they made up a special language that only I could understand…that they *spoke* to me. When I entered the main room of the temple, my eyes lighted on the sacrificial table. The stones shone brightly – the power of them awesome and terrifying.

Without warning, a large block of the wall started to shift sideways. It made a horrible noise, grating along the floor, wobbling and trembling like the glowing stones did. Eventually it came to a halt, and I stood at the opening of a pitch-black corridor.

Don't be afraid, Benedict. This is the only way.

I hesitated before taking the first step. My body was being compelled to go forward, but a small spark of my own fear screamed at me to turn back. The whispering increased. Now it didn't sound like one voice, but many, all urging me forward. I took the first step, and then the next.

My hands touched damp stone on either side of me, making a sick revulsion churn in my stomach, but there was no other way to keep my balance. Without them, it felt like I was entering a great, endless abyss of darkness.

I kept walking, the pathway seeming to go on forever, with no end in sight. I stumbled a few times, my body so tired it could barely keep me upright. Time passed, but I had no way of knowing how much. It could have been hours or minutes, but eventually I saw flickering lights ahead. I sped up as best I could, hoping that my journey would soon be ending.

The lights grew brighter. They were all the colors of the rainbow, bright pinks and greens and reds and purples. Hypnotized, I followed them, recognizing the lights as the stones that I had found in the castle.

I was getting close enough that the light was becoming blinding after so long in the dark. The stones spun and danced in their formations, swirling and blinking, calling me closer. I reached them, realizing that my path was blocked.

You can pass, Benedict... all you have to do is ask.

The whisper echoed along the tunnel, coaxing me on, but I didn't know *how* to ask. I reached out to touch the wall, seeing if it had a lock on it, or a handle—anything that would allow me to move it. There was nothing. Besides the stones, the wall that held them was smooth and featureless.

In frustration, I slammed a fist into the wall. A loud juddering noise seemed to shake the entire structure of the tunnel, and then the wall started to move. This time it was like the axis was in the middle of the wall. It spun around, leaving enough space on either side of it for me to slip through. I moved quickly, afraid that it was going to shut on me again.

As soon as I was on the other side, it thudded back into position, locking off the tunnel I'd just come from. I looked around. I was back in the castle. I recognized the narrow corridor, the crumbling walls and the cobwebs that decorated its corners. I started to run, my heart hammering—I was going to be okay…

Bursting through the wooden door, l landed on the other side, almost crying with relief to see the familiar red carpets and gray stone of Hellswan castle. I slammed the door shut behind me, and, without waiting a moment to catch my breath, I took off—headed in the only direction I could think to go.

I didn't want to see anyone.

I didn't want to try to explain.

I passed the emperor's room and then went further down the corridor, where another door would lead me down the stone steps and into the servants' quarters. A few surprised sentries glanced my way as I rushed past, but I ignored them, not stopping till I reached Ash's old room.

I climbed onto the bed, not bothering to change out of

my wet clothes. I grabbed the thin blanket and wrapped it round me, clutching the pillow tightly in my fist.

I lay there, shaking, and praying that I would stay awake.

Ruby

We traveled back on Ash's bull-horse, soon leaving the bright sunshine of Queen Trina's kingdom for the gloomy clouds that loomed ahead. The clouds seemed to be thickest in the distance, above the Hellswan kingdom.

"Home sweet home, right?" Ash smirked.

I chuckled grimly, wondering why Hellswan always seemed to be so constantly gloomy and drab—it was a stark difference from the kingdom we'd just come from.

"Was it always like this?" I asked Ash.

"Gray?"

"Well, yeah, I guess so."

"Always," he said. "You might see some of the other

kingdoms in time—none of them are like Hellswan. I don't know why it's like that. The old villagers, the ones I remember as a kid, always used to say that it was plagued by a great evil... I always thought they meant Jenus," he mused, laughing. "But as I grew up I realized that Jenus was a product of Hellswan's misery, not the cause of it."

I leant my head back against Ash, enjoying our last few moments together in solitude before we returned to the castle and the hordes of human kids that populated it. The sway of the bull-horse was making me sleepy, but I fought my tiredness, watching the landscape go past, content for a while.

"Are you going to think about coming back with me to the Seraq kingdom?" Ash asked me softly, his warm breath skating across the top of my head.

"I can't, Ash," I murmured. "You know I can't leave Benedict or Hazel. And I want to continue looking for Julian—he's got to be out here somewhere."

Ash didn't reply, but I knew he understood.

"Will you think about it?" he asked eventually.

"I'll think about it," I agreed, knowing that I would never reach a different conclusion. I wanted to be with Ash, and I hated the thought of abandoning him to Queen Trina's kingdom alone, but I couldn't leave my friends.

Especially with Julian gone. We needed to stick together.

The valley flattened out on the horizon, and I could see the start of Hellswan village in the near distance.

"Almost there," Ash sighed.

I took one of his hands off the reins and pulled it toward me, wrapping it more tightly around my waist. I wanted to make the moment last as long as I could. Tonight Ash would be packing, and tomorrow he would be leaving me. I didn't even want to think about it.

As we reached the first house of the village, there was a huge clap of thunder. It startled the horse, but Ash managed to calm him just before he broke into a canter. I looked up at the sky; it looked like the heavens were about to open.

"Great," I murmured.

The first drops plopped down, one hitting my head, and then the other landing on the back of my hand.

"Eugh!" I cried out. "It's *red*!"

Ash grabbed my hand, looking at it intently.

"That's weird," he muttered.

The rain started to cascade down, coloring the pathway and the houses either side in a bright, bloody crimson.

"What *is* this?" I asked in disgust.

"Probably pollution," Ash replied, though he didn't

seem entirely confident in his assessment. Neither was I—as a girl who had been brought up in The Shade, weird weather like blood-red rains didn't mean *anything* normal or good.

"Do you think we should wait it out?" I asked, looking at some of the barns either side of us longingly.

"I don't know...it doesn't seem to be anywhere close to stopping."

I looked up at the dark thunderclouds above us. He was right—it wouldn't be subsiding anytime soon. It was so dark that it looked like the middle of the night. All around us we could hear doors and shutters slamming against the rain, and the panicked cries and yelling of the village inhabitants as they realized what was happening.

"Hold on tight," Ash announced. "I think we just need to get to the castle as soon as possible, and get out of this. It might be poisonous for all we know."

I clutched at the saddle tightly as Ash dug his heels into the flanks of the bull-horse.

We raced to the castle, the clattering hooves spraying the red water everywhere, drenching me to the bone.

Ash slowed to a trot as we approached the portcullis. It was up, which was strange, but perhaps there had been such an influx of sentries seeking shelter that they'd just adopted an open-door policy for the evening.

Before walking over the bridge, Ash descended, taking the bull-horse by the reins. I looked up at the castle; every single light seemed to be blazing—it was the first time I'd seen the place actually look busy and like a fully operational castle.

"What the hell?" Ash yelled from the portcullis.

"What's up?" I asked, jumping down.

"There's a damn barrier up, that's what!" Ash kicked the air angrily, and I saw a slight tremor ripple where there shouldn't have been anything.

"What? Why would they put up a barrier?" I asked, confused.

"I don't know!" Ash flung his arms in the air in a gesture of helpless frustration. "Just because they can?"

He pushed at the borders again.

"Open UP!" he hollered.

I went back toward the bull-horse and picked up some small stones by the start of the bridge. I walked back up to Ash, and handed him a few.

"See how high the borders go," I suggested.

We both threw the stones into the air as high as we could. They bounced back. The border appeared to cover the whole of the castle.

"This is Tejus," Ash roared, "that stupid Hellswan *bastard*."

"I don't know, Ash. Hazel would kick up a storm if he did something like this, and why would he want to put borders up around the castle? We're not under any threat, are we?"

"Of course not," Ash replied. "But I'm sure he has his own, selfish reasons for doing so."

With a grunt of frustration, Ash headed back toward the bull-horse.

"What are we gonna do?" I asked, joining him. "Can you not call someone like Jenney, like through a sentry mind trick?"

Ash shook his head.

"I can't do that through the barriers. I can't even use True Sight. Nothing works. It blocks off everything."

He started to pace up and down, then stopped and looked up at the sky.

"We should head back to Queen Trina," Ash said, turning back to me with his arms folded.

I opened my mouth to say something, and then thought better of it. I didn't exactly relish the thought of spending the night in a barn, and at least in the luxury of the Seraq kingdom there would be hot baths, clean clothes and some food.

"Fine," I stated, inwardly groaning at the lack of appealing choices we had. "Let's go."

Ash lifted me back on the bull-horse and climbed on behind me. I already felt exhausted by the thought of the return ride.

Why on earth were those stupid borders in place? Had the ministers revolted or something, leaving Tejus and Hazel unable to do anything to remove them? I didn't like the thought of Hazel and Benedict locked inside that castle one bit…and I liked the thought of being at the mercy of Queen Trina even less.

Hazel

When I reached Tejus's rooms I slammed the door shut behind me, my chest heaving with painful gasps. I was soaked through. As I looked down at my robe and hands, it looked like I'd just been part of a mass slaughter, everything covered in streaks of red which was starting to turn sticky—just like blood.

Needing to get clean, but too worried about Benedict to think straight, I stumbled over to the windows that provided a view directly over the courtyard. Torches had been lit along the walls of the castle, though they flickered as they tried to stay alight beneath the torrents of rain. Tejus was still out there, shouting orders at the ministers as they all stood in a line, clasping hands while they tried to lift the barriers.

I looked out toward the forest, but it was just a great big lump of black and I couldn't distinguish a single tree, let alone hope to catch sight of my brother. I couldn't believe that Benedict had done something so stupid and reckless. Yes, he was a teenage boy and could be immature at times… but this? It wasn't like him at all. Obviously Julian's disappearance had hit him hard, and I tried to keep in mind that had it been Benedict missing I would have behaved in exactly the same way…and if it wasn't for the barriers, I'd be out in the forest myself.

Reluctantly moving away from the window, I left the living room to have a bath. The hot water was blissful, but when I'd finished the entire tub was dyed red—but at least I was clean. I took a towel and wrapped it around me, not knowing what to do with my clothes. I left them in a wicker basket by the door, feeling sorry for the servants who would be doing the castle's washing over the next few days. It wasn't going to be pretty.

Back in my room I found some of the sentry outfits that I'd worn for the trials, slipping on some black silk pants and a matching shirt. I smirked ruefully in the mirror. Great. Tejus and I would be wearing matching his 'n' hers outfits.

I peered out of the window again, looking to see if they'd made any progress on the barriers. There were fewer ministers out there now, and the line looked much more jumbled—some standing, some sitting, a few leaning against each other in exhaustion. I watched as one minister toppled backward, unable to remain upright a moment longer.

Tejus started to wave his arms around. I didn't realize what he was doing until the ministers started to disband. He was calling for a break.

What? No!

Selfishly, I didn't want them to stop. I could see that they were barely able to hold on anymore, but I felt that this was partly their fault. Had they known more about the entity, been just a little more cautious about a malevolent power they had supposedly locked inside their castle, then none of this would have happened. We would be home by now.

A few moments later, Tejus came into the living room.

"They had to rest," he announced, before I could say anything.

Tejus looked just as bad as I had—the only difference being that I had looked like the victim of some hideous slaughter, whereas Tejus looked more like the culprit. It appeared as if he'd been swimming in blood, not an inch of skin spared, and his black-red hair hanging in sodden tendrils by his face.

"I know," I replied, sighing. "I saw some of them fall—but they'll go back out again, right?"

"They will. It might be easier when the rain stops."

"I take it you think the spirit is causing the rain?" I asked.

He nodded, his face grave.

"I also think that this is going to get worse before it gets better."

"Do you mean the other plague stuff that was mentioned in the book?" I asked, my voice tight.

"Yes."

Which meant we had the 'fires of ice' and the 'pestilence of silence' still to come, thanks to the mysterious spirit that had helped lock the entity up in the first place.

"We need to find the stones," I murmured, placing my forehead against the coolness of the window pane. It was our only chance...without them we were next to useless.

"I need to take a bath," Tejus muttered. "Then I suppose we look through the books again, see if any of the ministers were more helpful than the lot I currently have."

I was about to vehemently agree when something caught my eye outside.

"It's Ruby, and Ash!" I cried, banging on the window. Tejus strode over and we watched as the two stood in front of the portcullis, unable to get through. Even from this distance I could see Ash's fury as he waved his arms around up at the castle.

"We need to go to the roof!" I realized my banging wouldn't be heard over the noise of the storm, and getting to the entrance of the castle would take too long.

"And say what?" Tejus asked, grumbling, but he was following me out of the room and up the steps that led to the tower.

I wasn't actually sure what we would say, but as long as Ruby knew I was safe then that would be something. Maybe she and Ash could keep an eye out for Benedict— or search for him in my place.

I thundered up the steps, and when I reached the entrance to the tower I leaned as far as I dared over the parapet and called down to them as loudly as I could.

"RUBY!"

I waved my arms around, hoping that if they couldn't hear me, they might see me at the very least. The wind carried my voice away, and neither of them looked up to the tower.

"Are there torches here?" I asked, looking around to see if there was anything I could throw down to the courtyard.

"Hang on," Tejus replied, disappearing back down the stairs.

I continued calling, but it was pointless—I was too far away.

A second later, Tejus returned with a lit torch that hissed and fizzled in the rain, and as I was about to throw it down to the ground, Ash and Ruby started to walk away.

"We need to go down! Quickly!" I yanked at Tejus's arm.

"Hazel, they've gone."

Argh!

I banged a fist against the stone parapet in frustration. Why couldn't we catch a break? I was drenched to the bone once again, and the small window of opportunity that had opened to me was now closed.

We descended the staircase in silence. I wondered why I'd been making so many wrong judgment calls lately—I felt like every time Nevertide and the sentries threw up a problem I did my best to overcome it, but always ended up falling short. I desperately wished that my parents and the rest of the GASP team were here; they could help. At least one of our team probably even had knowledge of creatures like the entity and the other mysterious creature that had locked it away…and they wouldn't be running around like a headless chicken, letting their emotions get in the way, especially their romantic ones.

"Do you think the books will have more answers?" I asked skeptically when we reached the living room.

"I don't know. But I'm not sure what else we can do. The ministers don't know anything helpful, and the one person who could have helped us is dead," Tejus stated.

"The emperor?"

"He's the only one who had access to the book. He must have known where the stones were kept, especially if our theory is correct about him removing one of them to help Jenus in the trials."

I mulled over Tejus' words. He was right. The emperor would have known everything, but I also thought about how unlikely it would have been for him to keep it all to himself. If none of the ministers had known, maybe he had confided in Jenus? Or even…

"Tejus, are you *sure* your father never mentioned the entity to you?" I asked suddenly.

"Of course I'm sure," he replied with frustration.

"Not even as a kid? There wasn't a sentry boogeyman

that all the kids were warned against?"

He gave me a puzzled frown. "I'm quite sure—but I'm not clear what myths and stories would do to help us, even if I could remember anything."

"Because they're often based on truth, in my experience, anyway. Your father might have divulged important information, but being a kid you would have ignored it."

"So what if I have? It still doesn't help us."

"It does!" I came to a standstill in the middle of the hallway. "We can do what you did when I was attacked by Queen Trina—look through your memories to see if there's anything that might be able to help, details that you might not be able to remember otherwise."

"I think there is a very small chance of this proving fruitful, Hazel."

"We don't have many other options," I stated firmly.

Tejus rubbed the back of his neck, drawing his hand away in disgust when he encountered the sticky blood residue. Even like this, half-drowned and disheveled, Tejus's appearance made my heart skip as he tried to stare me down.

"I don't think it's a good idea," he replied eventually.

"Why not?" I shot back.

"Because it's a waste of time."

"You don't know that. Why don't we give it a try, and if it doesn't work we'll return to the books—or if you have any other ideas…?" I smirked, knowing full well that he didn't have squat.

He was silent for a while, his jaw flickering in agitation as he deliberated. I didn't really understand what his problem was, or why there was such a role reversal all of a sudden. Usually it was Tejus who was eager to mind-meld, and I was the reluctant one—always with something to hide.

"Let me bathe first. You too." He pulled at a tendril of my freshly bloodied hair, moving it behind my ear.

"Okay," I breathed.

As I watched him stalk off to the bathroom, I wondered what Tejus was trying to hide from me. I couldn't see any other reason that he'd be so reluctant. I didn't believe him when he said it was a waste of time. There was a small chance that we might find something, and that was better than no chance at all.

Hazel

We sat opposite each other on the velvet sofas in Tejus's living room. Both of us had changed clothes, and we sat with damp hair from our baths. My mood had changed from one of hopelessness to a cautious optimism now that we were taking action—doing something other than reading the long-winded memoirs of clueless ministers.

I felt a mild sense of déjà vu. We had sat in almost the exact spot the day that I'd first managed to project my mind to Tejus, after Queen Trina had attempted to kidnap me. That day had ended any unnecessarily painful mind-melds with Tejus—he had no longer needed to go rummaging around in my brain, and instead our connections had taken on a far more pleasant quality... some of them really pleasant. I blushed, and cleared my throat.

"Okay, shall we start?"

Tejus raised an eyebrow. "I'm ready. Are you?"

"Yeah." I shook away the errant thoughts, and tried to keep my mind clear to receive whatever memories Tejus was able to share. I closed my eyes, waiting to feel the familiar feather-light touches of Tejus's mind reaching out to entwine with mine.

I waited for a moment, but I couldn't feel anything. I opened one eye, looking to see what the hold-up was. He was gazing at me, a perturbed expression on his face.

"Tejus?" I prompted.

"Sorry," he replied curtly, not sounding remotely sorry. "I'm ready."

I pursed my lips, and closed my eyes again. His reluctance was starting to become mildly offensive...and I wondered if he truly did have something to hide from me.

A moment later, I felt his mind reach out and touch mine. I focused on his energy, trying to draw it closer, and soon our bond became strong—in my head, an image of a thick, bright gold rope seemed to stretch between us, steadily becoming thicker and more dense.

Suddenly I was transported to a hallway of Hellswan castle. It was bright outside, and light flooded in from the large floor-to-ceiling windows. Tejus was with his brothers—Danto, Ferros and Jenus. All dressed in their black robes, with dark hair, they were difficult to distinguish, but I recognized Tejus instantly as the tallest. They were all waving wooden swords about, stabbing each other, but then laughing uproariously. Tejus had just been knocked to the floor, dragging one of his brothers down with him, when the group fell silent.

The emperor, looking much younger but just as imposing as I remembered him, glared down at his children.

"What is the meaning of this?" he roared at them.

"Sorry, Father." Tejus stood, dusting off his robe. "We were just playing."

The emperor yanked the sword out of Tejus's hand.

"You sword-fight with the masters, with steel. It is *never* a game. You are all Hellswans! When you waste your time with games, you degrade our name and put your own pleasures first. Jenus—what is wrong with that?" he demanded, turning his icy glare to the red-faced boy.

"Because duty to the kingdom comes first," Jenus whispered.

"All say it!" roared the emperor.

"Duty to the kingdom comes first," the boys chorused.

"Good." The emperor nodded. "To the study hall with you all."

The boys filed off, and the emperor watched them go.

As fascinating as the little interlude was to me, it didn't help us in the slightest. I tried to reach out to Tejus, to tell him to focus on the task, but I knew from personal experience that it was much easier said than done. I wondered why that particular memory had found its way to the front of his consciousness, but before I could focus on my own thoughts, I was planted in another of Tejus's memories.

He was with his brothers again, but this time they were in the emperor's chamber. A beautiful, raven-haired woman was sitting up in the bed, smiling at the boys as they lounged on the giant bed, occasionally pushing and shoving one another for space. Though beautiful, she looked unnaturally gaunt—the nightgown she was wearing drowned her frame. I realized that it must have been Tejus's mother before she died. I'd never asked how it had happened, but clearly she'd had some sort of wasting sickness. *How sad,* I thought, and as I did so, a slight blue tint filtered the color of the memory, tainting it with my emotion.

"Tell us the one about the man who flew!" Danto cried out.

"No!" Jenus replied. "I want to hear the one about the maiden who stole the sword, and died in the lake!" His eyes gleamed at the gruesome horror, and I wanted to scoff—interesting to note that Jenus was a complete psycho from a young age.

"I have a gory story." Their mother laughed at them. "Perfect for the heirs to Hellswan…but no nightmares, agreed? It's just a story," she reminded them, squeezing Ferros's hand.

"You're such a baby," Jenus hissed at his brother, but Ferros ignored him.

"Once upon a time," their mother started in hushed tones, "there was a handsome prince who lived in a magnificent kingdom—his land was vast and bountiful. The sun always shone, and his people lived in peace. His father was away at sea, fighting for riches and land in other worlds, far, far away. He was gone for so long that the people of the kingdom feared that their king would never return. Though the prince was sad, he agreed eventually to become king—and he would take a queen, the prettiest in all the land. For years they lived together in peace and harmony, and the queen begot a beautiful boy."

"This doesn't sound scary at *all*," Jenus moaned.

"She's getting to that part!" young Tejus interjected, punching his brother on the arm.

"Boys!" their mother exclaimed. "If you don't behave, you won't hear the story. But Tejus is right. I *am* getting to the scary part… One day," she continued, "the new king received a letter from his father. He was overjoyed, because it meant his father was alive. In the letter, the old king urged his son to come and join him in a new kingdom that he had discovered—an entire land that was theirs to claim. The new king made haste, packing his belongings and preparing all the people of his land to travel with him. The king and his family, and all the kingdom, traveled across the waters on great ships—hundreds of them.

"After several days at sea, they landed on the shore of his father's land. There was much celebration and joyfulness as the old king and his son were united at last. The new king was happy, but he encountered a strange sense of unease that pervaded his father's castle. When he questioned his father about it, the old king told him that the castle held a malevolent entity within its walls. When the old king had arrived in this new land, he had been enslaved by hideously disfigured creatures, as had the army of men that he had traveled with.

"After years of plotting, the old king and his men orchestrated a revolt, and managed to overpower the creatures with the help of a magical wispy demon—not quite man, not quite air—who locked the evil creatures away with magic stones.

"The new king was amazed at the story, but praised his father for all that he had done to overthrow the evil. Peace continued for a while, and the people settled into their new land. Until one day, when the new king's son came to him, saying that he had found a beautiful stone in the wall. The new king admired the stone, and then sent his son away so he could focus on the matters of the kingdom.

"That night, the wife of the new king came to him, saying that she couldn't find their son. The guards were alerted, and the entire castle was searched high and low. There was no sign of him, until one of the kitchen boys went down into the store rooms, and saw the young prince hanging from the rafters—his face almost entirely eaten and the bright stone still clasped in his hand.

"The old king announced that it was the work of the entity, who had now been released. The skies went dark, and the entity's army rose from the dead. They massacred the villages and all the people of the kingdom, including the handsome new king, whose eyeballs they ate off silver platters, and the old king's hand—which they hung from the door of the castle, to remind all who might travel their land just how deadly they were.

"Can anyone guess what the land might be?" she asked, laughing at the horrified faces of her sons.

"It's Nevertide, isn't it?" Tejus asked in a whisper.

"It is indeed…and what's the lesson in the story?" she asked again.

Silence descended over the boys as they tried to work out the point of the story.

"The boy, he shouldn't have taken the stone?" Tejus asked.

Their mother nodded and smiled.

"No one must take the stones of Hellswan castle, or the immortal one will rise from his prison and gobble you all up!"

"Where *are* the stones?" Jenus asked, open-mouthed.

"Ha! That would be telling." The emperor had walked into the bedroom. "I don't want any of your curious minds walking around the castle looking, do I?"

The image flickered and faded.

I expected the mind-meld to come to an end, but another image appeared instead.

No longer tinted by the blue, the colors of the image were saturated with a bright yellow light, making the scene before me seem hyper-real. I couldn't make out what he was showing me for a few moments, but then I could make out two figures sitting on the thrones from the coronation ceremony. I couldn't make out who they were, but then the image flickered, and the perspective changed, so I was standing right in front of the thrones.

It was Tejus and I, sitting side by side and holding hands, smiling at one another. I thought for a moment that it was the memory of Tejus's coronation…but then I realized that *I* was wearing a crown. I waved and smiled at the cheering crowds in front of me, and then Tejus leaned over and kissed queen-me.

What?

The image jolted and spluttered, and suddenly it was cut off, leaving just a blackness in my mind. The connection had been broken.

What was that?

I opened my eyes to see my surprise mirrored in Tejus's expression, and a faint red coloring his cheekbones.

"My mother's story." He spoke abruptly, his voice hoarse. "Was it of any use?"

Oh, okay… so we're going to ignore that, then…

"Um, yes, I think so," I managed, my mind still trapped on the last image.

"Hazel!" he snapped.

"Right. Um…" I racked my brain to make some sense of the story. "Well, the wispy creature—the one that was half man, half air—that sounds like a jinni to me."

"A what?"

"A jinni. They're sort of like spirits or fae, they live in a land called The Dunes, in the supernatural realm… Do you know if they've ever inhabited Nevertide?" I asked.

"No, not that I know of. I've never heard of these creatures," Tejus replied, his brow furrowing.

I guessed that wasn't too surprising. I still didn't know exactly where Nevertide was, but even if it was located in some hidden area within the supernatural dimension, jinn tended to keep to their own territory.

"How much of the story do you think was true?" I asked, wondering how much of the tale was a warning to her young boys, made up to scare them into not touching the stones.

"Well, we know that the stone prison is true," Tejus mused. "I think the rest was a warning…what concerns me is the 'armies' my mother spoke of. If that part of the story is true, then it is not one malevolent creature that we're facing, but an entire horde of them."

I nodded slowly.

This has quickly gone from bad to worse...

"Do you recognize the description of the entity? Is it something you've come across before?" Tejus asked.

"There wasn't exactly much to go on," I replied. "It could have been anything—it just sounds like the stuff of nightmares."

I thought of the young boy taking the stone, and thought of Benedict. An image flashed in my mind of my brother hanging from the rafters of the store room, and I shuddered, feeling like throwing up.

"Okay, plan B." I stood up, refusing to dwell on imagined horrors when we had enough real ones on our plate. "Do we have one?"

"Search the castle from top to bottom." Tejus shrugged. "Right now I can't think of anything more we can do. It all leads back to the stones, and without locating the lock, we don't know for certain that one has gone missing...or how we close it again."

"Okay. Can we also put a guard outside—to speak to Benedict when he comes back?" I asked quietly.

Tejus hesitated, and I interjected before he could open his mouth.

"He has the stone."

Tejus nodded, clearing his throat. "Consider it done."

For the first time today, I was glad that Benedict was out of the castle. I didn't want him and the stone anywhere near here…If the story from Tejus's mother had taught me anything, it was that this place was dark and consumed by evil—it had always been so, and probably always would.

BENEDICT

I must have dozed off for a while, because I woke up with a start, looking around Ash's room in a blind panic till I realized that there wasn't any danger, that I was safe for the time being. I waited for my heartbeat to regulate, and then staggered up off the bed.

All I could think was that enough was enough. I couldn't remember exactly what had happened last night after I'd stumbled in the forest. Just flashes of the weird temple, the green light and the stones blinking at me, dancing in the dark. I had to speak to someone about what was going on. I had spent days living in mind-numbing terror, becoming afraid of shadows, afraid of closing my eyes—afraid of what I could see as much as what I couldn't.

But without Julian here, there wasn't really anyone I felt comfortable talking to. Ruby and my sister would just be worried—the last thing I wanted was for them to stop focusing on finding Julian and lowering the Nevertide barriers. I wanted to go home. That was all that mattered.

I thought of Yelena. She had promised to help me with this earlier. Maybe speaking to her would help, and if she was willing to stay up and watch me, then perhaps things wouldn't feel so bad, and at least I would know for sure that I hadn't done anyone else any harm.

With shaky steps, I followed the passage through the servants' quarters up to the ground floor of the castle. There were a lot of ministers wandering around—a lot giving me odd looks, which I didn't understand till I caught my reflection in an old mirror. I was still covered in the red rain from the forest, having completely forgotten to remove it when I'd got to Ash's room. *Whatever.* It would have to wait.

There weren't any guards outside the human quarters, so I let myself in, cautiously poking my head around the door first, checking that Ruby and Ash weren't there first.

I didn't feel like facing a barrage of questions about where I'd been.

A quick scan of the room reassured me. There were a couple of kids lounging around, looking bored and tired, and Yelena standing by the window at the back of the room.

"Hey, Benedict." One of the kids smiled up at me sleepily. "You look *weird*."

I nodded absent-mindedly in return, not wanting to stop and chat. Yelena had spun around as soon as my name was called, and was staring at me as if she'd just seen a ghost.

"What?" I said, my eyes widening as I approached her.

Without saying a word, she clasped onto my wrist and dragged me through to my bedroom—her grip was surprisingly strong for such a little thing. Once we were in the room, she slammed the door behind her and glared at me.

"Where have you *been?*" she stormed.

"You know, I was looking for Julian," I replied, confused by her angry tone.

"Everyone's been worried sick! Your sister came down looking for you—she's petrified something's happened to you!"

I groaned. "Yelena, please don't tell me you told her where I was?"

"I had to!" she cried angrily. "I don't even know how you even got back in here."

"What do you mean?" I asked.

She rolled her eyes in exasperation.

"The barriers! They've been put up around the castle now. No one can get in or out...well, we *thought* no one could get in or out—obviously you did. How can you not know any of this?"

"I fell asleep in Ash's room," I said, waving aside her question. "What do you mean about the borders? Are there *more*? Who put them up?"

"No one knows." Yelena shook her head. "No one will tell me anything."

"Well, I need to tell you stuff," I replied, recalling the reason that I'd come to see her in the first place. "All you have to do is promise that you'll try to believe everything I say, because all of it is true—I swear."

Yelena plonked herself on the bed next to me. "Oh, don't worry about that. I don't think anything's going to shock me anymore, not after this. I'll believe you."

Taking a deep breath, I told Yelena everything. From the moment that Julian and I had found the narrow corridor in the castle, and how only I had been 'allowed' down into it. I told her about the whispers, the late-night walks, the Viking remains and the temple, the stones, wondering why everyone seemed so tired all the time— wondering if I'd had anything to do with it, and if I was somehow to blame for Julian's disappearance.

To her credit, she listened to the whole thing without saying a word. The only thing I left out was standing over *her* body. I didn't want to freak her out more than she was already, and judging by her half-open mouth and wide, wide eyes, she was well and truly freaked out.

"Benedict, you're right. I'm so out of my depth here…this stuff…it's *terrifying*."

Yeah. Saying it all out loud had made me more aware of just how wrong everything was. When it was all in my head, it was easier to lock some of the stuff away and just try to get on with the day, pretending that the voices talking to me were somehow good, that they were helping me in some way. Now that it had been said out loud, the ugly, evil truth was out. Whatever those voices were, they were *not* trying to help me.

"We need to speak to your sister and Ruby," she whispered again.

"I can't. It will just worry them, and then I won't be

allowed out of their sight...they'll lose focus on the borders. Trust me, it's better this way."

"Benedict! Maybe it's better if they won't let you out of their sight—it sounds like you're in real danger."

I slumped back on the bed. I didn't really have the energy to argue with Yelena, but I honestly dreaded telling my sister. Maybe I could go and see her later, and then decide whether or not she should know—if she was stressed and preoccupied with the borders, then I wouldn't tell her.

"Okay... I'll go and see my sister. But will you still keep your promise about watching me while I sleep?" I asked.

Yelena looked down at me, worried and forlorn.

"I'm frightened," she whispered.

I nodded.

"Yeah, me too."

Yelena reached over and took my hand. For a second I wanted to shake it off and tell her not to be so silly, but it was actually comforting to finally have some human contact... it felt safe.

"I'll do it," she confirmed.

"Thanks," I replied, words not really able to convey how grateful I was to her.

We sat on the bed in silence for a while, both frightened, both feeling a bit lost and, in my case, thinking about how utterly sick I was of Nevertide.

Hazel

Tejus had done as he'd promised. There were two guards waiting outside by the gates to the castle, watching for signs of my brother. It was difficult to tell what time it was; the clouds hadn't moved and the rains hadn't stopped—it could have been early morning or the middle of the night for all I knew. I hadn't been able to get any sleep. Tejus had brought up books from the library, and so his living room looked like a study hall with books piled up on every available surface, most discarded because of their uselessness. The ministers and any available guards were conducting a thorough search of the castle.

According to Tejus, the ministers had kicked up a fuss

about this, telling him that they wouldn't be able to touch the stones if they did find them—reminding him that it was the jurisdiction of the emperor. I couldn't believe how bloody-minded they were being. If Tejus's mother's story and the snippets we'd been able to glean from the ministers' chronicles were to be believed, we were all in mortal danger, and the ministers were fussing about the small print. At least Tejus and I were completely aligned for once—he had returned from his meeting with them looking murderous. We were both more than happy to ignore the rulebook in order to stop the entity.

While I watched the blood-splattered courtyard, my mind would occasionally drift to the image I'd seen in Tejus's mind. He'd made it perfectly obvious that he didn't want to talk about it, but it had lodged in my mind. Of course it had—he'd shown me as his queen! I couldn't just shake it off in the same way he could.

I was stunned by what I'd seen. The rational part of me believed that the image made perfect sense. Tejus would be looking for a wife now that he was king. That's what royalty did, wasn't it? And I shouldn't take it too seriously. It was little to do with me per se, and more about making a power play—*putting the kingdom first*, just like he'd always been told to do.

But my heart felt differently — wildly, breathlessly separate from my head. I hoped that Tejus was falling for me in the same way I felt like I was falling for him. We had met in such unbelievable circumstances, and overcome so much together—fought and tried to beat every obstacle that was in our way, rescued one another time and time again—that I couldn't really imagine a world where Tejus wasn't around. I didn't want to.

Which was right—my head or my heart—I didn't know.

There was a knock on the door. I ignored it, letting Tejus open the door, thinking that it would be ministers or guards with another pointless update, them having found nothing and suggesting another plan was made, but then having no suggestions as to what else we could do.

"Hazel, it's for you," Tejus' deep voice announced.

I spun around and saw my brother standing in the doorway, coated in the red rain, looking as white as a sheet, but here. Alive. I ran across the room and held his body tightly, unable to speak for a few moments as I felt how frail his body was, how cold.

"Benedict…" I gasped, my raw throat holding me back from saying anything more. Tears threatened to overflow, and I forced them back.

"Hey," Benedict replied. "Sorry I went off into the forest. I didn't mean to worry you."

I shook my head, breaking away to look at him. "It doesn't matter—as long as you're safe."

"I am." He smiled weakly.

"How did you even get in? There are borders up all around the castle. We thought that no one could get in or out." I looked up at Tejus, hopeful—maybe they had come down on their own?

"Yeah, Yelena told me. I think I came in before they went up…I went to Ash's room and fell asleep there."

"Why Ash's room?" I asked, confused. It seemed like a strange thing to do, especially as he'd obviously not bothered to shower either.

"I was just tired. The kids make a lot of noise."

"Okay. Do you want to sleep up here tonight?" I asked, desperately wanting him to agree.

"No, it's fine. Someone needs to keep an eye on them." He shrugged. "Ruby and Ash aren't here either. Are they locked out because of the borders?"

I nodded.

"I saw them try to come in, but they couldn't. I'm pretty sure they're okay though." I smiled, even as I reassured myself. "Probably off in some barn somewhere. Ash will take care of Ruby."

I wanted to reassure Benedict too, but he grimaced at the mention of the barn. I was about to ask what was wrong when Tejus cleared his throat.

Right. The stones.

"Benedict, do you still have the stone I gave you? We need it back. We think it might have something to do with the barriers."

"Oh, sure," Benedict replied, digging around in his left pocket. Then his right pocket…then his back pockets. His eyes widened with panic, and he gulped. It would have been almost comical under any other circumstances. He checked his pockets again, going back to the left pocket…and then he stopped.

My heart sank.

I didn't dare look at Tejus.

"I think…I've lost it," he breathed.

"Could it be in your room?" I asked, trying not to panic just yet.

"No…I never removed it from my jeans…I—I could have sworn…" His sentence trailed off, and he looked as if he were about to faint.

"Benedict, i-it's okay," I reassured him, reaching out to comfort him again. His entire body was shaking, which seemed like an extreme response. I realized that I'd put my brother under a lot of pressure. Too much. Too much for just a kid.

"This is all my fault—not yours, I promise you." I looked dead straight into his eyes so that he would see the truth of what I was saying. "The stone was my responsibility; I should never have let it out of my sight."

Tejus growled from the back of his throat.

Crap.

I needed to get my brother out of here before Tejus exploded.

"Why don't you take a bath up here? I've got clean clothes you can wear."

"Yeah, thanks," Benedict agreed, still looking like he was stuck in his own world of guilt and fear. Feeling helpless, and not knowing what to say to make him feel better, I showed him to the bathroom and left some clean sentry clothes for him to wear.

Feeling sick, I returned to the living room.

Tejus was standing by the windows, waiting for me.

Here goes.

"I know what you're going to say," I started, before he could talk. "But it's not his fault."

"I know," Tejus bit out. "I don't blame him—I blame

you."

I nodded, rubbing my forehead, trying to think what we were going to do now. I had been hoping that the stone would have somehow led us to the rest of them…or, at the very least, we could have shown it to the ministers to see if they could discern whether it was one of those that trapped the entity.

"How could you have been so reckless?" he asked.

"You know I had no idea what it was," I replied. "If this is anyone's fault, it's your father's and his *stupid* labyrinth trial's. If it is one of the stones that belongs to the lock, then it was him who removed it in the first place!"

"You are so frustrating!" Tejus exploded.

"So are you!" I snarled back. I meant that with every cell in my body—I wasn't just referring to the stone, but literally everything else about Tejus.

I slumped against one of the sofas, looking dejectedly at the books littering the room. I didn't want to have another argument with Tejus about the stone—what was done was done. Yes, I'd been stupid, but I hadn't known. Right now the important thing was trying to find a way to fix it…but how?

"I guess we hit the books again?" I asked.

"I don't have any better ideas," Tejus fumed.

He marched back over to the coffee table and started flicking through the books with the short, staccato movements of a man who was well and truly pissed off.

"Hazel?" Benedict called from the door of the living room. He was clean and dressed in the fresh clothes I'd put out, but still deathly pale.

"How are you feeling?" I asked, walking over to him. We stood out in the hallway, away from Tejus.

"I'm okay… tired. I think I'm going to go back downstairs now," he told me, but looked longingly inside the living room of Tejus's quarters.

"You're more than welcome to stay, you know that, right?" It was probably Tejus putting him off staying up here.

He shook his head, now looking toward the stairs.

"I need to go," he said quietly.

"I'll come down with you."

We made our way back to the human quarters, Benedict silent the entire way, but walking close to me—obviously needing some kind of comfort. When we reached the rooms, most of the kids were already asleep. Yelena was sitting up on the sofas, curled in a blanket, her eyes fixed on the door. She smiled in relief as we approached.

"You look better," she said to Benedict.

"I feel better."

She nodded, her expression more somber and concerned than I'd ever seen it.

"Did you tell Hazel about the—"

"Not yet!" Benedict interjected loudly.

I looked at them both, wondering what was going on. Benedict looked sheepish, while Yelena just looked mad.

"Anyone want to tell me what's going on?" I asked, unnervingly sounding like my mom for a moment.

"It's nothing…just that I almost got attacked by wolves in the forest, but it was fine in the end."

"What? Why didn't you tell me?" I exclaimed.

No wonder he was so pale and shaken. He must have been utterly terrified.

"Sorry, didn't want to worry you, and like I said, I'm actually fine. *Yelena* was overreacting."

"No, she wasn't." I glared at him. "You could have got yourself killed! I know you're worried about Julian, we all are, but running off into forests isn't going to help anything."

"What happened to 'I'm just happy you're safe'?" he asked mischievously.

I rolled my eyes at him, "Don't push your luck. And come on—bed, you need to get some sleep."

He huffed, but made his way over to his room without saying goodnight to Yelena. The girl looked at me, opening her mouth like she wanted to say something. She hesitated, and then she smiled halfheartedly at me.

"Night, Hazel," was all she said.

"Night, Yelena. And do tell me if he decides to make any more boneheaded decisions, please."

"I will." Her reply was firm, but her eyes darted quickly to the shut door of Benedict's bedroom, no doubt worried about what *he* would do if she ever told on him. I shook my head as I left the room, so relieved that Benedict had come back in one piece.

The loss of the stone wasn't great for us, but I was relieved that at least Benedict no longer had it. The story about the young prince hanging from the rafters flashed into my mind again. It was just the stuff of grim fairytales, but even so, I felt better with Benedict well away from it.

The new anxiety that was starting to play on my mind was that if Benedict didn't have it... then who, or what, did?

Hazel

When I re-entered the living room, Tejus was in the same place that I'd left him, poring over the books. The candles and torches in the room were lit, casting a warm yellow light over everything. He shut one of the volumes abruptly as I approached and he stood up, turning to face me.

"Hazel, I have an apology to make. I do realize that this is not entirely your fault. I should have realized that the stone was potentially more dangerous and potent than I assumed—my father never did manage to stick to the straight path."

Whoa.

The apology was sure unexpected. As I'd ascended the

staircase, I'd been preparing *mine*, not for a moment thinking that Tejus would admit wrongdoing.

"Thank you. But I own my part—leaving it with Benedict was probably one of the stupidest things I've ever done in my life. I'll probably always regret it."

Tejus nodded slowly, lowering his eyes to the floor as he rubbed his hand along his jaw.

"Yes, but you did it for me."

Suddenly the room was thick with tension, and I felt color rising in my face. My stomach tightened as I realized the truth of his words—well, the half-truth. It wasn't the whole picture.

"And to ensure the barriers were raised." I smiled crookedly, trying to break the atmosphere, suddenly afraid. Afraid that Tejus would start realizing how I felt about him, and I didn't think I was ready for that yet...not till...

Not till he tells you first.

"That image that you saw...the one in my mind. I want you to forget it," he said brokenly.

"Uh..." I swallowed hard. "I don't think I can." I found myself closing the distance between us, trying to make him look me in the eye. "I don't know what it means. What was it, Tejus?" I dared breathe.

He groaned softly before replying.

"An idea I once had—a foolish one, something that can never be."

"What do you mean?" I whispered. "Why?"

"For reasons I can't explain. I hardly understand it myself, but I need you to trust me that it's for the best. Whatever was happening between us, it just can't."

His answer didn't make sense. But I didn't know why I expected anything else. Tejus was clearly determined to remain an enigma, keeping me shut out. This was the second conversation we'd had about *us*, and I still didn't understand where I stood—or what he was keeping from me.

"Look me in the eye and tell me," I said, "that you don't want anything to happen between us—that you don't feel anything for me. That image was me sitting beside you as your *queen*. How on earth do you think I can just brush that aside?"

"Because it's what I had to do!" he burst out.

Our eyes locked. His were black, the pupils drowning out the irises of his eyes, and all I could see in his expression was desire—hot, urgent and completely consuming him.

I took a step closer toward him, but his hand shot out

to stop me, grasping my hip, keeping me at arm's length.

"Don't, Hazel," he whispered, flinching.

He was silent for a moment, trying to keep himself in check. "I'm sorry that I'm making no sense," he said after drawing a breath. "Will you just please believe that this is as difficult for me as it is for you?"

"I'm sorry, but I can't believe that," I replied, trying to keep my own voice steady.

"But it's the truth. You being here—having you as a…friend—has altered me fundamentally, Hazel. And I will never be the same again, with or without you."

"I… I'm not sure that I want to be without you," I replied, holding my hands across my stomach, trying to keep myself whole while I felt like I was breaking apart.

"The price is too great, Hazel. As soon as this is all over you will return home, and you'll feel differently. You're young—"

"That is so patronizing!" I ripped the words from my throat. "You can't tell me how I will feel or what I won't feel—you don't have that right."

He swallowed. "You are right. I am just trying to make this easier…"

"Well, don't."

I took a step back and briefly closed my eyes, trying to

calm down. But all I could think was that somehow I had fallen in love with him. I didn't know when, and I didn't know why, not when there were so many reasons to stay away, but it didn't change the fact that I had. I had abandoned myself in the worst possible way, and I was out there alone on the ledge—Tejus just wasn't willing to take the risk and fall with me.

"I'm going to the library," I whispered hollowly.

Tejus removed his hand from my hip, and he seemed to relax a fraction.

"No, it's warmer here. I'll go…I want to look at some blueprints of the castle's foundations as well."

I nodded, not caring either way. I just needed space.

"Please stay here," Tejus said quietly. "The castle isn't safe. I don't want you to go wandering off."

"Okay." I wasn't going anywhere in this state.

The door shut quietly behind him, and the tears I'd been holding at bay started to run down my face. I brushed them aside angrily, determined to continue looking at the books.

If Tejus could shut off his emotions and get on with the job, then so could I.

BENEDICT

As soon as Hazel left, Yelena came into my room looking sheepish.

"Sorry," she muttered. "But you did say that you would tell her everything."

"She was already worried out of her mind, and now Ruby and Ash can't get in the castle, Tejus was going mental about the stone—which I've *lost* somehow…it just seemed like a bad time," I replied defensively.

"What do you mean you lost it? Is this the stone that Hazel gave you to look after?" Yelena asked.

I had told Yelena all about the stones, the ones in the creepy secret corridor and the one that Hazel had given me…which had looked very similar.

"Yeah," I replied quietly. "I'm not sure what I've done with it."

Yelena fiddled with the corner of the bedspread.

"Benedict, is it possible that in these…blackouts you keep having, you left it somewhere?"

"That's what I've been thinking," I replied despondently. "I have flashes of memories – like holding the stone out in my hand, seeing it glow or whatever in front of me on some weird table in the Viking Graveyard, but also seeing more stones in the castle, in a tower – I don't really know everywhere that I've been…and I don't even really know where the graveyard is!"

"Did you tell Hazel that?" she asked.

I shook my head.

"I didn't want to worry her. I don't want her to know about this…stuff. Not until we find a way to fix it."

She thought about what I was saying for a few moments, then turned to me.

"Maybe the stone won't be that hard to find. Maybe when I follow you tonight, you'll lead me right to it?"

"Maybe," I replied. I didn't feel as optimistic about it as she did. "Are you still prepared to do that?"

"To follow you? Yeah. I am. Something bad is going on

here, and I guess it's up to us to get to the bottom of it—especially since Ruby and Ash aren't here anymore, and there's another stupid border up."

As frightened as Yelena was, I could detect a hint of excitement in her voice. I would have been the same in her position, but I needed to warn her that it wasn't the right response. When I was in those 'blackouts,' as she'd called them, I wasn't in control of myself. Anything could happen—and none of it good.

"Be careful," I warned her. "Remember to follow me only at a distance. Don't interrupt me or approach me, okay? And if I start…hurting anyone – or anything like that, just knock me out, all right? Take one of the swords with you."

She stared at me solemnly. "I promise that I will, and I'll be careful."

I nodded, knowing that she wasn't taking my warning as seriously as she should be. But I didn't know what else to say, and I was desperate enough not to try to scare her off the idea.

"Well, I guess we just wait. It shouldn't take me too long to drop off." I could already feel my eyelids starting to droop.

"Okay. I got some weird drink off Jenney earlier—she

said it was a sentry version of coffee. It tasted gross, but I feel wired."

I nodded, but Yelena always seemed pretty hyper to me. I couldn't really tell the difference.

"Should I wait outside?" she asked.

"Yeah," I agreed. So far I hadn't tried to jump out of any windows, so I assumed that I'd be safe on that front.

"I could stay in here though?" she continued. "Watch you while you sleep—see if you say anything?"

No, thanks.

"Um…I don't think that's going to help me fall asleep," I replied. "It's better if you wait outside."

"Okay!" She leapt up off the bed. "See you in a bit."

"Just remember what I—"

"I know, I'll be careful."

Yelena left the room, leaving the door open. I rolled my eyes.

"Yelena, can you shut the door?" I yelled.

"Okay, okay!" She darted back and closed it firmly.

"Thanks," I called out.

I made myself comfortable in my bed, glad that I wasn't going to have to do this alone, but it didn't mean I wasn't any less terrified about what might lie ahead.

* * *

Here again?

The bright lights of the stone wall danced in front of me. They seemed to flicker more brightly than I'd ever seen them before—in a way, the stones looked as if they were *happy*, like little sprites twinkling and dancing for me.

There was a dull pain in my left hand, and my palm felt damp. When I looked down at it, I realized that my hand was bleeding profusely. What the hell had happened there? I didn't remember cutting it or anything, but there was a bright red gash carved deep into my skin.

I looked at it for a moment, and then lowered my hand back down to my side.

It wasn't as important as the stones—it didn't really matter.

Hypnotized, I stared at the wall, trying to discern a pattern, but as soon as I thought I was following one, it would change and I would become even more transfixed—drawn even further into their mystery, their power and the deep, strong magic that they held.

The patterns seemed to be drawing me to one stone in particular. It was a bright, brilliant, pink stone, almost neon in color. While I watched, it started to vibrate just as

I'd seen the other one do. Soon it had wormed its way out of its socket and dropped on the floor with a sharp clang. I watched as the stone moved across the floor toward me, rolling over, again and again, till it touched the tip of my shoe.

Pick up the stone, Benedict. The whispering started again, and my body went cold with fear.

Pick up the stone...once you get the stones this will all be over...

I tried to fight the impulse to reach down and pick up the waiting stone. I fought it with every bone and muscle in my body. It wasn't enough.

I bent down, and my fingers brushed its bright surface. It was warm to the touch, as if the energy inside it was alive—pulsing through to my hand, driving me to curl my fingers around it, carrying it safely in the palm of my hand.

I stood upright, knowing that I wasn't done yet—the voices still wanted something from me. I placed the stone in my pocket, its presence almost feeling reassuring. On some level, it felt good to be close to that much power again.

While I stood motionless, waiting, the wall started to move. It slowly grated on its axis, just like it had done the night before. Ahead was the dark corridor that would lead me to the Viking graveyard.

No! Please not there again! I called out to the voices.

But you must, Benedict. You must.

One foot moved in front of the other, and I crouched down to get through the narrow opening. My skin was drenched with sweat, and it kept falling into my eyes, blurring the tunnel in front of me.

I kept walking along, my fingers brushing the damp stone, the only way I could guide myself. The door shut behind me, and when it did, the hold of the voices seemed to lessen momentarily, and I became more aware of what I was doing. There was something I needed to remember…something good in all this—something that was going to save me, but I couldn't quite remember what it was…

Yelena.

Something she was doing…what was it?

I couldn't remember, and soon I was lost in the depths of my own fear again—an endless trudge through a black tar of horror that seemed like it would never end, that I would be stuck, frozen in the darkest place in my mind, forever.

HAZEL

Every time thoughts of Tejus came rushing up to meet me, I tried to shove them back down, locking them away so they wouldn't drag me down into a more depressed and morose state than I already was. I had been looking through the books for hours, and now the text was swimming before my eyes as I fought back tiredness. I'd found nothing even close to helpful, just a bunch of boring records of ministers' meetings, usually on the topic of dividing up land and ensuring that they had enough grain supplies for winter. Seriously dry stuff.

If I'd had more stimulating reading material, I felt like my plan to block out all things Tejus-related would have worked a whole lot better, but as it was, the price of a century-old ton of grain wasn't really doing the job.

I couldn't concentrate.

It was all too frustrating.

Maybe if I'd had a better idea of what was going through his mind, I'd be able to put all this behind me…or at least be able to understand the situation. From what I could make out, Tejus did have feelings for me but wasn't willing to admit them, which made the entire thing more frustrating. Or maybe he *couldn't* admit them for some reason. *Is he promised to someone else?* I wondered. It hadn't occurred to me before, as I'd never noticed any other women around Tejus—other than Queen Trina, and that was obviously over—but he was a royal. Perhaps his father had arranged for him to marry a princess in some other kingdom?

It was one theory, but it didn't explain some of what he'd said to me. What had he meant about the *price being too high?* That didn't fit with my theory…unless if anyone found out he'd be in trouble. That did seem likely. If any of the other kings were as odious as Tejus' father, I could imagine his head being on the chopping block if he wasn't faithful to Hellswan's traditions.

Or…

I was making up stupid stories. I needed to actually talk to Tejus, to find out what was truly going on, rather than to continually try to second-guess him. Though having an honest conversation with Tejus didn't seem to ever be an easy task.

I was starting to reopen yet another weighty tome when the door to Tejus' room swung open, bashing against the wall behind it. I jumped up, startled, and spun around to see Yelena standing in the doorway, bent double and gasping for breath.

"What's the matter?" I rushed forward, hoping to see Benedict behind her. When he wasn't, my heart skipped a beat.

"It's B-Benedict," she gasped out. "You've got to come!"

"Where is he?"

She couldn't speak, just gestured for me to follow her and took off at a run. I kept pace with her easily, not daring to ask what was wrong or where my brother was. As Yelena speedily navigated the hallways, desolate rooms and corridors of the castle, I was stuck in my own private nightmare, my imagination flitting from one horrific scenario to the next, always coming back to the image from the gruesome fairytale of the young boy holding the stone, gently swaying from the rafters.

Get a grip! I commanded myself. I was getting close to hysterical and it was the last thing that anyone needed, especially if Benedict was in trouble.

Yelena came to an abrupt halt at the start of one of the corridors. She took a moment to catch her breath, and then slowly started to walk to the other end.

"It's this." She pointed to one of the walls.

Written in the brown-red pigment of already drying blood, a sentence had been scrawled across the wall in large, jagged lettering. It read:

"To follow me is death. But I shall come. I shall come back to claim you."

"Who wrote this?" I gasped. "What's it got to do with Benedict?"

She glanced at me, and then returned her gaze back to the wall.

"He did," she replied in a hollow voice.

What?!

My body stiffened suddenly, and I placed my hands across my stomach. I felt physically ill.

"Yesterday, before he went off to the forest, he told me that he had been sleepwalking—all over the castle, outside, everywhere. He had been hearing voices, but other than that he couldn't remember what happened while he was sleepwalking, only the whispers and the stones—bright, gleaming stones that he said were calling to him.

"I said I would follow him, and we'd find out what was going on, where he was going…maybe also find the stone that you gave him, the one he lost. I'd followed him before, but it had always freaked me out, so I'd run back to the room. But I promised him I'd follow him this time." She looked at me with desperate, pleading eyes. "I promised him! And so I did. When he came here, he cut his own hand with a dagger—I don't even know where he got it from—and started to write on the wall. I started trying to speak to him, to tell him to st-t-top…"

Yelena broke down into sobs, and I held her tightly, feeling my heart thud in my chest with fear.

"What happened next, Yelena?" I coaxed the girl gently, trying to repress the urge to scream.

"He didn't stop. He just stared at me, but not really seeing me, you know? Then he walked down here."

Yelena untangled herself from my arms, but took my hand and walked forward, leading me further down the hallway to what first appeared to be a dead end. Yelena pointed to a wooden closet door on the right-hand side of the wall.

"He went in there, and I tried to follow him, but I couldn't. I broke my promise."

Her face was a mask of utter misery, and as frightened as I was for my brother, I needed to comfort the girl who had tried to save him.

"Yelena, i-it's okay. You were afraid. Anyone would be."

"No!" she cried. "It's not that. You don't understand. I *can't* follow him—the corridor is blocked, by some sort of boundary. I can't get in…only he seems to be able to."

"What do you mean? Like a sentry boundary?" I asked, opening the door. I could see nothing ahead but pitch black, and my fear for my brother reached levels of hysteria.

"Yes, try it," Yelena replied. "You can't go further than a certain point."

"Wait here."

I walked over to one of the flaming torches and grabbed it from the wall. Holding it aloft, I stepped into the small corridor, ducking my head as I travelled along its narrow passage. Yelena was right. When I reached a certain point, the space in front of me seemed to form an elastic barrier— I could feel it stretch like a rubber band as I tried to move past it, but no matter how hard I tried, it would not give.

"Benedict!" I called out into the passage. "BENEDICT!"

Only my own echo greeted me, sounding like it was taunting me for my vain efforts to reach my brother. I wondered what the hell this passage was. Where did it lead to? It looked like an endless tunnel, with no lights in the distance, just nothing but an empty void of space. How would my brother have felt walking down here, all alone? I felt sick just thinking about it.

"Yelena?" I called out, making my way back.

"I'm here!" she shouted.

I came to the entrance, and peered out into the light of the hallway.

"Do you know where the library is?" I asked.

"Um…yeah, I do."

"Tejus is there. Will you go and get him? Say I need him to come right away."

"O-Okay!"

I watched her run down the hallway, and then I marched up to the other end and back again, collecting all the torches that I could manage to hold. I laid them down in the narrow corridor, not able to leave Benedict while he was down there, and desperately wanting light to mark his way home. Who knew how long that passage would be?

Or if it veered off in different directions?

Sweat was pouring down my back when I finished. The hallway was in near darkness, but the others that led from it provided just enough light to see the writing on the wall that Benedict had left.

My brother did that?

I couldn't believe it. It might have been him physically, but it sounded like my brother's mind had been taken over completely. I didn't know what on earth had done such a thing, but I knew that I had helped it. Yelena's mention of the stones made me believe that somehow Benedict was connected to the entity, to the hidden locks, and I had given Benedict the key to making that connection possible...

I sat waiting in the passage by the barrier, looking off into the black nothingness ahead. I wanted him to come back. I wanted the words on the wall to be true. *I shall come back to claim you.* I didn't care what he came back for—as long as he came back.

HAZEL

"Hazel?"

I heard my name being barked from the end of the corridor by a familiar voice. I had sat down on the cold stone floor while I watched and waited for Benedict to return, but now I stumbled to my feet, running along the passageway.

"Tejus?" I called, fumbling out of the closet door and tripping over into the hallway.

He grabbed me in his arms, holding me tight against his chest as I sobbed. In that moment, I didn't care about us. I didn't care what we were, or what we might never be—I just wanted the comfort that, in the absence of my brother, only he could bring me.

"It's all right," he murmured against the top of my head. "It's going to be all right."

I didn't believe him. My brother might come back as he'd promised—but would he be coming back as Benedict, or something else? It felt like the only thing that was keeping me together was Tejus's arms and his solid, safe presence… a complete change from the last few hours, where I'd thought that he was the one breaking me apart.

Gently he released me, letting me step back a little, but still within the confines of his embrace.

"You need to tell me what happened," he commanded gently.

I looked over at Yelena, and she nodded. I wiped the tears away from my eyes and took a deep, shuddering breath. I told him everything that had happened, Yelena filling in the details. Hearing it again, in the form of a cold, factual account for the sake of Tejus, nearly sent me over the edge. Somehow it sounded worse, like it wasn't my brother that we were talking about, but some strange, evil creature—a mindless thing. I showed him the writing on the wall, and Tejus looked at it, his face carefully expressionless as he acknowledged the threat contained within them.

The entire time we were explaining, he remained touching me in some way—taking my hand, or holding his palm lightly against the small of my back. It helped me feel less alone.

When we had finished, Tejus walked back to the narrow passageway.

"Wait here for me, please. I don't want you going in there alone again," he said, as he crouched down as far as he could to get into the doorway.

"But Benedict—"

"I know," he interjected, "but it's not safe."

I stood back, allowing him to go in alone. I leaned against the other side of the hallway wall with Yelena, and we waited for Tejus to re-emerge.

"How are you holding up?" I asked her softly, taking her cold, small hand in mine.

"I want to go home," she whispered back to me, leaning her head on my shoulder. "I'm frightened."

I nodded, not knowing what to say to comfort her. Maybe just listening was enough. I was profoundly grateful to Yelena, that she'd done what she had—following him, all alone, when it must have terrified the life out of her. I wondered if the message on the wall was specifically for her, and hoped to God that it wasn't.

Yelena moved closer toward me. "If I fall asleep, you won't leave me here, will you?"

"No, of course not," I croaked. "Go to sleep. I'll wake you if anything happens."

Tejus was taking too long already. Why hadn't he come out? As Yelena curled up in a ball on the floor, I approached the doorway and peered into the depths—just in time to see Tejus, hunched down and walking toward me. I took a step back to let him pass, and he emerged from the passage.

He straightened up, his face thoughtful and preoccupied for a few moments before he focused on me, raising his hands to gently squeeze my upper arms.

"Hazel?" was all he said. But the question asked a million unsaid things like, 'how are you holding up,' 'what do you need,' and most importantly—'do you trust me?'

"What's the plan?" I asked shakily. I could tell that Tejus was thinking something through, that he had an idea forming in his mind he wasn't entirely sure would work.

"If Benedict can cross that castle barrier, it means there's a break in it," he muttered, releasing my arms and beginning to pace up and down the hallway.

"What does that mean?" I asked.

"Sometimes, when sentries create barriers, their intention is to have the ability to pass through them when no one else can. To do this, they must create a break in the barrier—a place where it can be opened and closed repeatedly," he replied.

I nodded. "I get that, but obviously we can't open it, can we?"

"Alone, no, but it's the weakest area of the barrier. Think of it like a piece of ceramic; one hairline crack, no matter how small, and the entire creation is fallible. I believe that if we use all of the ministers we have available, and my guards, we will be able to open the barrier around the castle."

This was good news. If the barriers re-opened, we wouldn't have to wait for Benedict to return—we could go out and find him ourselves.

"Let's do it," I said. "How long till we can start?"

"There's one drawback. We will need to wait for Benedict to reappear—it's the only way that we can be sure we'll be attacking the barrier when it's at its weakest," he replied, warily waiting for my reaction.

"But we have no idea when he'll be back!" I cried. "We don't know for sure if he'll even be back. What if he can't get through again?"

"We have to assume that his threat to return is genuine—and as the human child said, this isn't the first time that he has done this, and he's always been back before." Tejus sighed deeply, and looked away from me. "If an entity of some kind is controlling him, then I have no doubt that he will be able to re-enter the castle. He's obviously being used to manipulate the stones in some way."

The thought made me feel sick—but only because it was being voiced for the first time...I had also thought it was likely that it was the entity who was controlling my brother. I just didn't want it to be true. Though our reading hadn't helped us much with the details, the one thing that all the dead ministers had agreed on was how truly powerful this creature was.

Tejus continued to pace up and down the hallway, still ruminating on his plan.

"What do we do in the meantime?" I asked quietly.

Tejus glanced over at Yelena, fast asleep on the floor.

"We gather everyone here—and we wait till Benedict shows himself. But..." He hesitated. "If the ministers are going to have the best chance they possibly can, they need more energy. They've been working on the barriers for the last twelve hours, and they are all drained. I was thinking that perhaps we could use the human children…for the ministers to syphon off them."

I froze, not entirely sure whether he was joking or not. *Of course he's not.* After my initial, kneejerk reaction, I knew in my heart that I would agree to this—I would agree to whatever it took to save Benedict…but those kids. They'd already been through so much.

They'll never go home if the barriers aren't opened, I thought. It was true, maybe, but we hadn't even really begun to look at alternative options. Was it absolutely necessary for them to experience the pain of syphoning, after they'd been promised they'd be safe now? An idea flickered into my mind.

"Say I agree to this," I said slowly. "I want to teach them—the kids and the ministers—to do it the way that you and I can, throwing their energy out, so it doesn't hurt so much."

Tejus looked at me, raising his eyebrows. "I'm not entirely sure that's going to work—I don't know if they will be able to manage that the way you can."

I shook my head. "It's worth a try at least, and these kids have been chosen because of their strong minds, just as we were. They know enough about the supernatural world now to have had their minds broadened."

He still looked doubtful.

"Tejus, I don't want to put them through any more pain. Please," I begged.

Eventually Tejus smirked.

"Hazel, do you ever only think of yourself?"

I was stunned by the question. I had thought that so many of my actions lately had been selfish—putting my needs before others, especially my brother's.

"I do, more than you know," I whispered back.

When it comes to you, I am completely selfish.

"I find that hard to believe," he murmured, looking into my eyes. His eyes looked hooded and dark, and for just a moment it was only Tejus and I in the hallway, the rest of the castle and my problems a million miles away from here.

"You don't know me well enough," I replied, my breath hitching.

"You're wrong. I see you, Hazel Achilles." He smiled sadly. "Sometimes you're all I see."

I stared at him, a tight fluttering in my chest that stopped me taking a breath. After a beat, he averted his gaze and cleared this throat.

"We will teach them, I promise. I'll call them all here. It won't take long," he reassured me.

"I'll collect the kids," I replied, readjusting my head space swiftly—away from Tejus—and refocusing on the task ahead of us.

TEJUS

I had never felt less in control.

I might have been crowned as ruler of Hellswan days ago, but it meant next to nothing. Whatever this 'entity' was, the creature had me incapacitated—helpless against its power, not even able to leave my own castle. My people were at its mercy, and the red rains were only the beginning of the horror that we would face. I had witnessed my father rule this land, and the rest of the kingdoms, for decades of peace; then I had taken the crown and Nevertide had descended into disruption and darkness. Had my father had the presence of mind to speak to my brothers and I about the entity—to put his ego aside for just a few moments to tell us that his land was built on fragile standing, that we were potentially on borrowed time—I would be able to forgive him now. But as I raged against the entity, I raged against my father in equal measure.

A traitor to his people.

That was his epitaph. All I would remember of him. He had betrayed us all—and I was left to clean up the mess.

I thought about what Hazel had said earlier, about Jenus possibly knowing more about the entity than I did. It wasn't unlikely. As soon as the borders around the castle were down, I would seek the wretched shell of my brother out in the hope that he had answers.

It wasn't just in my role of king that I felt helpless.

Since the night of the coronation, I had vowed to push Hazel away, to make it clear we had no future, nothing that we could possibly share. Then I would see her for just a moment, she would say something, make me want to laugh—and all my willpower would crumble to dust, and I would find myself transfixed. Unable to shut out the constant pull toward her, like an eternal orbit, circling one another until one of us would relent and in a moment of honesty we would grow closer, making it even harder to turn her away the next time.

"They are all ready," one of my guards announced.

I turned away from the window to see the hallway full of sentries all sitting, cross-legged, in a line through the hallway. Behind them, the human children sat with their backs against the wall. They all looked pale and small, and I could hardly believe that these were the chosen tools of my competitors in the trials.

Hazel stood by the entrance to the passageway. More torches had been placed inside to line the dark tunnel, and their glow flickered across her pale skin. Her dark hair gleamed with hues of gold and red from the flames, and suddenly I could believe that she originated from supernatural beings. I had never seen a creature so otherworldly, so heartbreakingly calm in the face of her sorrow.

I walked slowly toward her, not wanting to disturb her till I had to.

"Hazel?" I interrupted as I approached.

She turned her large eyes up to meet mine. They were red-rimmed and her mouth was tightly pinched as she tried to hold her emotions in check. She had never looked more beautiful.

"They're ready. We should begin." My voice was hoarse, and I clenched my fists at my sides to repress the urge to take her in my arms and offer what little comfort I could.

She nodded, and I turned to the waiting sentries and children.

"You all know why we're here. The borders can open tonight, with your help. However, we will need the help of the humans in order to accomplish our task. In return for their help—willingly given"—I smiled briefly at the little blue-eyed girl who had followed Benedict and been instrumental in rounding up the assistance of the children—"I want them to have the least painful experience possible."

The ministers started to whisper among themselves, as predicted.

"There is a way," I insisted. "A way for the humans to push out their energy voluntarily, for you to receive. Not only is it less painful for the humans, but the syphoning is also far more effective when they're not in pain and trying to resist."

There was silence for a while, and then Lithan spoke.

"We are willing to be taught," he announced, and the rest of the ministers nodded their agreement.

"Good. Hazel and I will provide a demonstration."

I turned to Hazel, and she gave me a small smile.

"Thank you," she whispered, out of the ministers' hearing. "I know you didn't have to."

I nodded, feeling uncomfortable taking her gratitude. Had it not been a more effective method of syphoning, I probably wouldn't have.

"Let's take this slowly," I murmured back. "We should try our hardest to stay here so we can continue to give instructions. Do you think you can?"

"I'll try," she affirmed.

I gestured for her to sit down, and I positioned myself opposite. Our fingers brushed as we moved closer in the now cramped space of the hallway. I clenched my jaw, and briefly shut my eyes to shut down the instantaneous effect she'd just had on every cell in my body.

"Hazel starts," I announced to the group, "and pushes her energy out toward me."

"It's like meditating," Hazel informed the group. "Try to get rid of all the thoughts in your head, pushing them outward. Try to picture the person you're going to be partnered with, and send whatever's in your head toward them."

I felt her energy fill up the space between us, and then I mentally reached out to grasp onto it. I explained what I was doing as best I could. Never having had to put any form of syphoning into words before, it was difficult. What was I to say? *It's like coming home, like having an anchor when you thought you were the only being in the world unbound to another.*

"Try to visualize the bond," I murmured to our audience, "as something solid and unbreakable."

I marveled at how easily Hazel and I could now practice this. The 'rope' that we habitually visualized formed strong and vivid almost instantly. This was the point when we would usually vanish into one another's memories, but I tried with everything I had to stay in the present, and I could feel Hazel doing the same.

Hold on, Hazel.

I kept speaking to the sentries, and I could vaguely hear her doing the same thing—the soft murmur of her voice started to meld with mine. I could feel myself slipping away...

An image flickered in my mind. It was of Hazel. She was standing on the tower of the castle, the wind whipping at her hair and her dress. She was looking at me and smiling. The landscape behind her was bright, clear blue skies and fresh, easterly winds that brought the smell of pine with them. Hellswan hadn't looked like this in a long time, not since before the death of my mother.

This is wrong—get back...

I didn't want to. I stepped toward her, inhaling her scent among the forest's aroma. I was lost. She opened her mouth to say something, but though her mouth formed the shape of words, no sound came out. I moved closer, brushing my hands around her waist to pull her closer. She stopped smiling, staring solemnly up at me.

"I wish I could save you from myself," I whispered to her.

"You can't," she replied. "It's too late."

I traced one of my hands up her spine and grasped her hair, pushing her face upward to meet mine. Our lips met. Her mouth was warm and silk-soft, and she tasted like apples. I groaned, wrapping her closer toward me, utterly unable to let her go. Our kiss intensified, my body pushing toward hers as her fingers wound around the back of my neck. Her response prompted a heady mix of lust, desire and urgency to completely consume her—there would never be enough time in my lifetime to get my fill of Hazel.

The image started to flicker, the stone of the tower starting to shake beneath our feet.

Hazel broke our kiss.

"We have to return," she breathed.

"I can't."

She smiled at my echo of her own words a few moments earlier.

The image juddered and spun, the tower seeming to crumble as the skies of Hellswan turned black. The connection was broken, and an icy reality washed over me.

I opened my eyes to see the familiar hallway and Hazel seated on the floor, looking at me, horrified, her cheeks bright red. I dared turn my face toward the waiting sentries, but they all just continued to look at us with polite interest.

I cleared my throat.

"So, that is how it is done... Are there any questions?" I asked.

"It appeared that your heart rate increased dramatically during the syphoning process—is that usual? Are we in danger of heart complications or extreme stress during the exercise?" Quentos's reedy voice cut across the silence.

I repressed a smirk, and felt Hazel's foot nudge mine angrily.

"It's nothing you can't handle, Quentos. The effects vary, you'll be fine."

A few more questions were asked on the logistics of the process—some from the ministers and guards, some from the older children, which Hazel answered, her blush slowly receding as she gave details of the syphoning in a detached manner.

Once the demonstration was over, I helped Hazel up to her feet and she allowed herself a small smile in my direction.

"I don't want to talk about it," she murmured.

"That makes two of us," I replied, as we walked away from the group. "You should get some rest. There's nothing you can do until Benedict gets here—both of us are going to be needed to open the barriers."

"I know, but I don't think I can rest," she muttered, chewing on her lip.

"You have to. You've been up too long. You can stay close—I thought you could use the Imperial bedroom." It was closer than both the human quarters and mine.

Hazel looked back at the group of sentries.

"Okay," she agreed.

We walked the length of the hallway, Hazel averting her eyes from her brother's words written on the wall, and then we continued in silence till we reached my father's chambers. I had asked the servants to light the fire earlier so that the room would be warm. Since his death I had visited the room once to look for the book the ministers had mentioned, but had been unable to find it. It seemed musty and stale, like the air had stayed still since its sole inhabitant had passed away.

"Will you be all right here?" I asked Hazel, wondering if she found it as claustrophobic as I did.

"I'll be okay… It's just weird being in this room."

I watched as she moved toward the bed. She gingerly sat on it, running her hands over the bedspread.

"Did you have any more ideas on the cause of his death?" she asked suddenly.

I hadn't thought about it in a while. There had been so many other distractions that I had abandoned my original investigation, which had led me to believe the kitchen boy was my key suspect, but I had been unable to find any conclusive evidence with which to pin him down and hold him accountable.

"I'm not sure. I suppose the entity is now a possibility," I mused out loud.

"You mean my brother?" she asked, her voice empty.

"It is not your brother, Hazel. Something is controlling him—and I doubt very much that your brother, even under manipulation, would have been able to end the life of the most powerful sentry in Nevertide."

She nodded, letting out a small sigh. Kicking off her shoes, she tucked her feet up under her.

"Are you cold?" I asked, moving to wrap the coverlet around her without waiting for an answer.

"I think it's just exhaustion…and shock, I guess."

She looked completely lost, drowned by the cover and the large bed. Sometimes I forgot her young age—it was easy with Hazel to think she was older than her years. She had been through so much since she arrived, and I sometimes wondered how she had the courage to keep her spirits up, to maintain an unwavering faith that she and her friends would survive this world and return to their own.

"I can't believe that Benedict didn't share any of this with me. It's been going on for so long—why didn't he tell me?" She looked at me wide-eyed, as if I would have the answers.

I had none to give her. I was so cut off from the nuances of emotion, human or otherwise, that I would hardly know where to begin.

"I'm sure he had his reasons," I muttered.

"I guess I was distracted all the time," she replied, her voice thick. "I should have taken the time to speak to him more, to check how he was adjusting to everything. He wouldn't have kept all that to himself…I just don't know how he coped. I'm a crappy sister."

I turned to her in astonishment.

"Hazel, you are an incredible sister. Ever since you arrived here you have put your brother first, above all else—your own life, my life." I thought of her attempt to murder me, and smirked. "No brother could have asked for more. It is humbling to see your love for him. It is something I doubt I will ever truly understand."

She looked taken aback by my speech. She remained motionless, gazing at me with the tears she'd been holding back slowly, soundlessly running down her cheeks.

I strode toward the bed, throwing caution aside, knowing that I would despise myself later. I only knew one way to provide her with some comfort—no matter how brief.

My heart felt like it was going to break through my ribcage as I stood before her, looking down at her small figure, the waves of her hair falling around her shoulders and her bright eyes staring up at me.

Walk away!

This will only end up one way. You will destroy everything that she is, everything that she holds dear.

"Please," she said. It wasn't with desire or want, but with need.

"It won't change anything," I replied hoarsely.

"I know," she replied.

I picked her up from the bed, holding her small frame against mine. Her arms wrapped around my neck, her legs around my waist till there wasn't an inch of space between us.

This time it was she who lowered her soft lips against mine. I could taste the salt of her tears as our mouths melted together. The kiss grew hungrier, more desperate. As much as Hazel needed to block out her current reality and the events of the last few hours, I found that without realizing it, I needed to do the same.

I needed to be with the creature I put above all else: the strange old soul I had fallen in love with, the woman I would put before my own life.

While evil waited for us outside, Hazel and I drowned in one another's kiss, knowing that facing the darkness could wait.

Hazel

Tejus had stayed with me for a while as I attempted to get some sleep. I had let my head rest on his chest, being slowly lulled by his heartbeat. Just as I was about to finally drift off, Tejus had been called out by a guard and left me alone in the room. As soon as he was gone, I tossed and turned for a while on the emperor's bed, but eventually gave in, staring at the ceiling while my mind whirled with the aftershocks of having my world turned upside down so completely.

The terror I felt for Benedict made me feel utterly hopeless, but I was also starting to realize that I wasn't alone in any of this. Whatever was happening between

Tejus and me, I knew that I could afford to fall to pieces and he would manage, somehow, to pick me back up again.

Something in him had changed since the night of the coronation. He was just as protective over me as he had always been, his demeanor just as harsh and impenetrable, but now it was occasionally tempered with tenderness. The more I thought about him trying to push me away—like telling me in our mind-meld that he wished he could protect me from himself, battling with himself constantly when I knew part of him wanted to kiss me—the more I became convinced that Tejus was trying to behave unselfishly. That he was trying to save me from something, maybe even himself.

If that was true, then Tejus had changed dramatically from the man I had first met, who had told me to never underestimate that side of him.

His own attempts to protect me from himself seemed completely misguided. I wasn't worried about what Tejus kept hidden behind his various masks of indifference and the walls that he put up to isolate himself from the rest of the world. I was only worried about not seeing him—being denied the chance to decide for myself who Tejus was, the bad and the good.

Tonight it was difficult to understand how I'd ever thought of him as cold and heartless. He had done nothing but try to help me, both practically in terms of getting Benedict back home, but also providing me comfort and kindness when I'd felt my absolute worst. I wouldn't forget it.

As soon as this was over and my brother was safe, I wasn't going to let Tejus hold back anymore. I was going to get to the bottom of what he was hiding from me—what he thought I so badly needed to be protected from. I loved him now, that much I knew, and I wasn't going to give up without a fight.

I heard a knock on the door, and Tejus entered. I sat up abruptly, ready.

"We think we can hear him coming down the corridor. It's time."

"Okay, let's go."

I tightened my robe around me as we left the emperor's room and hurried down the hallway. Tejus's frame was tense, and I felt my own body seizing up with anxiety as we moved closer to the passage.

The sentries and the kids were sitting where we'd left them, all cross-legged and upright, each human behind a sentry, with a few sentries gathered who didn't have human helpers. I also noticed some of the sentries from the servant quarters had come to join and help out. Jenney was sitting with Yelena, holding each other's hands tightly.

I moved to stand with Tejus at the entrance to the passage. I couldn't see anything yet, but as a hush descended, I could hear the faint sound of footsteps walking slowly toward us.

"This isn't going to hurt him, is it?" I asked Tejus.

He gave my hand a brief squeeze.

"No. All the power will be focused on the barriers," he promised.

I wanted to call out to Benedict, to run in there myself and drag him out of the clutches of whatever was controlling him, but I realized it would be pointless—and was more likely to scare him off in the opposite direction.

Come on, Benedict, I prayed. *Come back.*

I waited with bated breath as the footsteps got louder. Tejus's hand didn't leave mine. A few minutes passed and we heard the sound of heavy stone grating across the floor. I looked up at Tejus, who looked as surprised by the noise as I was.

"A door?" I asked.

"It sounds like it," he murmured.

The sound came again, but with a heavy thud that

sounded like it had closed shut. To my relief, the footsteps continued in their movement toward us.

"Are you ready?" Tejus asked me.

"Yes."

"I'm going to start syphoning as soon as we see him."

I nodded, not moving my eyes from the passage.

Soon my brother stepped out from the darkness. I could only really see his face, lit up with the light from the torches I'd laid down. It was ghostly white, and seemed to float disembodied through the gloom. His eyes met mine, but they were completely clouded and didn't even flicker with recognition.

Benedict!

At the same time as my brother approached, I felt Tejus's feathery-light touches to indicate that he was starting to syphon off me. I pushed my energy out to him as best I could, but my mind felt like it had been frozen in fear along with the rest of my body.

"Try to focus," Tejus whispered.

I was trying, but it felt like he was asking the impossible.

Benedict was moving closer, his lack of expression indicating that he wasn't even aware we were there. Behind me, I heard the deep breathing of the sentries—the effort they were using to push their energy forward and destroy the boundaries.

Beneath my feet I felt the ground tremor. It was light at first, but then it jolted and rumbled more loudly, and I could feel the gray walls of the castle creak and shift and then the sounds of ornaments falling—the smashing of mirrors, and light scatterings of plaster falling down onto us.

"It's going to collapse on him!" I screamed, starting to rush forward into the tunnel. Tejus yanked me back, gripping me around the waist.

"No, Hazel!" he roared. I fought him, but his grip only increased.

Benedict didn't even seem to realize what was happening, keeping his footsteps steady. The floor rumbled even more loudly, and I realized for the first time that I could almost see the barrier that had been built in the distance—it seemed to glow with an icy-blue light for a few moments, and then started to shake and rip, curling up into bright white sparks, like a tissue being set alight.

It's working!

Benedict was only a yard from the entrance. A few steps more and he would be safe.

"Benedict!" I cried out as more dust and debris poured down from the ceiling of the passageway. As soon as the last blue light was gone, Benedict seemed to regain control of himself. He looked around wildly, panting in shock as if he hadn't realized he was in the tunnel.

"Benedict!" I cried again. "I'm here, it's okay. You're safe!"

I lurched forward, angry that Tejus was still holding me back. There was no longer any danger, but Benedict had frozen, no longer moving toward me as terror seemed to sweep through his body.

"Hazel?" he cried.

"I'm here!"

My voice was drowned out by a sharp whipping sound as air rushed out of the passage, knocking me backward into Tejus's body. No sooner had it blasted out than it sucked itself back in with a giant whoosh, fluttering the cloaks of the sentries and pulling Tejus and me forward. He reached out swiftly and clasped the frame of the doorway to avoid us being swallowed up by the tunnel.

Benedict was digging his hands into either side of the wall, his nails scraping over the stone as the force of the air tried to pull him back to wherever he'd come from.

"LET GO OF ME!" I screamed, knocking my elbows back into Tejus's chest.

"Are you insane? No!" He pulled me back.

"I can't hold on!" Benedict groaned.

"You have to hold on, I'm coming," I cried back, tearing at Tejus, trying to force him to let me go.

My eyes met my brother's for a moment.

Hold on!

His eyes widened with shock as his fingers gave way and he was dragged back into the tunnel, his body disappearing back in to the darkness.

"NO!" The cry tore from my chest.

Just as abruptly as it had come the wind ceased, and the shaking of the castle settled down to tremors and then nothing at all. The hallway was left in a deathly silence.

I stood in the passageway, looking into the gloom, trying to comprehend what I had just seen. Eventually I could hear the sound of soft sobbing, probably coming from Yelena.

I couldn't cry.

I was empty.

RUBY

I took my time in the bathroom. It was easy to do; in the middle of the room stood a large mosaic bath, practically the size of a kids swimming pool, surrounded by pots of plants that were obviously flourishing within the humidity of the steam that constantly rose off the water. Dotted around the bath were plinths made of blue stone, which held towels and pots of scented oils, and one was carved into a low dip to create a hand basin. One side of the room was entirely made up of floor-to-ceiling windows overlooking the night's sky—which here was a navy blue covered in bright stars, completely devoid of the dark clouds that had overshadowed Hellswan.

I had spent hours in here already, scrubbing off the red rain that had seeped through my robes, and trying to remove the bone-cold feeling I had from traveling for so long.

As soon as we had arrived at the castle, we had been greeted by a minister waiting at the gates, as if he had known we were coming. I guessed they'd seen us approach, and had kindly prepared a grand room for us, with two adjoining bathrooms and a massive double bed…

Which was the other reason I was spending so much time in the bathroom. I felt weird sharing a room with Ash without really understanding why. We'd all shared a room when we'd first arrived at Hellswan, and a tiny little cubby hole at that. But it was slightly different now, I supposed, and as much as it would be nice to have some privacy with my sort-of boyfriend, it also gave me butterflies in my stomach.

"Did you drown?"

Ash's voice floated through to me from the bedroom, making me laugh.

"I'm coming out in a minute," I called back.

Hastily I pulled on the fresh robes that a servant had presumably left me. Once again in Queen Trina's kingdom, we hadn't seen a great deal of staff since we'd arrived back—just two ministers: the one at the gate, and another who showed us to our room in near silence, telling Ash that the queen would speak with him soon.

I stepped through into the bedroom, glad to be clean and warm once more.

Ash was sitting on a chaise longue in one corner of the room. He looked slightly uncomfortable, and I wondered if it was for my benefit that he'd avoided the bed.

"Hey, Shortie, welcome back." He grinned at me.

"Hey, yourself. Sorry I took so long… that rain was disgusting."

He shook his head. "I wish I knew what the hell was going on with that place—why would they put up barriers at a time like this? Something's not right."

I snorted. "There are a *lot* of things not right at the moment. Julian's been missing for ages now, the borders around Nevertide still haven't come down, and then there was that horrible goat…" My voice trailed off. I wanted to mention the nymphs I'd seen in the castle earlier today, but I didn't want to get into another disagreement about Ash taking the position of Queen Trina's advisor.

"Do you think there's a connection?" Ash replied thoughtfully.

"There usually is." I sighed. The one thing I knew about

the supernatural world was that things rarely happened out of the blue—there were always clues and signs that something unpleasant was bubbling under the surface. People usually ignored them till it was too late.

"I just can't work this one out," I continued. "There are too many elements. Too much I don't know."

Ash nodded. "I thought while I was here we could try to look up that symbol we saw in the barn, see if there's a reference of it anywhere. I'm assuming Queen Trina's got the same kind of library that Hellswan has—a bunch of history books written by dead ministers."

"That's a good idea," I replied. "But how long do you think we're actually going to be here?"

"I suppose until we hear that the borders have been removed. There's no point otherwise. You might as well try to get used to the place, Shortie. I know you're not happy being here, but we should be grateful we're not stuck in some damp old barn tonight."

He was right, I was grateful for our lavish surroundings, but it didn't stop me from feeling distrustful of the queen, or being slightly weirded out about the lack of inhabitants in the castle.

"I know…but don't you find it a bit unnerving that we never see a soul around here? I mean, how *safe* do you feel?" I asked cautiously.

Ash laughed.

"It's obviously just run very well. It's not like we're without anything. Maybe Queen Trina likes her staff not seen and not heard. It's not all that unusual. I feel safe here—safer than I ever did at Hellswan, and it's my home. And listen, if there is something weird going on here, or Queen Trina's up to no good, then better that we discover what it is." He smiled up at me. "I'll protect you, Ruby. You don't have a thing to worry about. I promise."

I raised an eyebrow at him. "That's a stupid promise."

"I'm confident."

"You're cocky," I quipped back, "there's a difference."

Ash rose from the chair and walked toward me. I didn't know what he was doing, and smiled at him uncertainly.

"I'm going to try something." He grinned down, standing right in front of me with only an inch of space between us. He took both my hands in his and wrapped them around his back, moving us closer. Suddenly, without warning, he lifted me up in his arms, cradling me as he walked back toward the chair. I giggled, nervous and feeling the same fluttering in my stomach that I'd experienced in the bathroom. He sat down, placing me on his lap.

"Right, we're going to mind-meld...but this time, instead of sharing memories, I'm going to try to send you some of my general calm. See if I can affect your mood that way."

I rolled my eyes. "We've been locked out of the castle and you're calm? Oh, please—I saw you screaming in a bloody rage at Tejus."

I could feel Ash smiling behind me, and he lazily wrapped his arms around my waist. "I'm calm now...Trust me."

My hands closed around his. I smiled to myself. I already felt slightly calmer and we hadn't even started yet. It seemed that in this instance, Ash's touch was enough.

"Oh, by the way," Ash murmured into my hair, "sleeping arrangements...I'm more than happy to sleep on the floor if that will make you more comfortable. I'm not assuming we're going to...you know."

I felt my face redden.

"No, uh, it's okay, you don't need to sleep on the floor. The bed's huge—we'll manage," I replied, grateful that he'd brought the subject up, even if I did feel super awkward.

"Just don't compromise my modesty, Shortie," Ash chided me.

I punched him playfully in the arm. "Shut up."

"Ready to be transported into my sea of calm?" he asked.

"I've got a better idea, actually."

I shifted in his lap and took his face in my hands, gently stroking the soft stubble across his jaw. I dipped my head down, kissing him chastely on the lips.

"You're right." He smiled. "That's a much better idea."

He tightened his arms around my waist, pulling me closer. Our lips met more forcefully, and I sunk into the dreamily familiar tastes and musk of Ash's body and mouth. My hands ran along the back of his thick shoulder blades, digging into his muscles.

Then we were interrupted.

A loud knock came from the door to the room. I sighed, shifting off Ash. He gave me a smirk, and walked over to open it.

The same minister who had escorted us to our room was waiting in the empty hallway.

"I'm sorry to disturb you, Ashbik, but the queen would like to talk to you." He smiled pleasantly, but didn't bother to glance in my direction.

"I'm coming," Ash replied, looking back at me and smiling. "I won't be long. Are you okay here, or do you want to come?"

"I'm sorry," the minister interjected, "the meeting is a private one. I'm sure you understand."

"She can wait outside," Ash stated firmly. "Ruby?"

"I'm okay, really—go."

"See you then." Ash's smile had dimmed, but he winked at me as he shut the door behind him.

Great.

It seemed that whenever Ash and I were in Queen Trina's castle we were separated at some point by her. I understood why Ash would be needed to speak with the queen—I was sure she would be interested in the rains and the borders up around Hellswan—but it didn't make me comfortable that I was never included in these. It might have been typical royal behavior, but I had observed that Tejus always fought tooth and nail to have Hazel accompany him wherever he went, leaving her out of very little. Why was Queen Trina so reluctant to have me in the meetings? Though I had no evidence, and a *lot* of bias after the conversation with Abelle, I couldn't help but feel like she was trying to drive a wedge between us.

Wow. You're starting to sound like a crazy jealous girlfriend...is that what you want to be? I asked myself in disgust.

I paced up and down the room slowly, not knowing what else to do. I felt too restless to get any sleep—worried about Hazel and Benedict, trapped in the castle, and also knowing full well that Hazel would be going out of her mind with worry about Julian, and now me. Even if we couldn't get into the castle, it would be worth visiting tomorrow as soon as it was light. We could at least get a message through the barriers, and I could see for myself that Hazel and Benedict were okay. Ash might think it was pointless, but I didn't. And the more I could get him to spend some time away from here the better.

A flash of light caught my eye, coming from beneath the doorway. It was so quick, I'd thought I imagined it, but pressing my ear to the wood, I could hear very faint footsteps walking in the opposite direction Ash had just gone.

I opened the door and peered outside into the hallway.

Up ahead I could see a glow of light, flickering in the dark of the palace.

Nymph.

This time I was determined to follow her and get some actual answers. I ran back inside the room and pulled on my shoes, then rushed back out—leaving the door slightly ajar so I'd know which one it was on my return.

I ran as quietly as I could along the hallway, going in the direction that I'd last seen the glow. Luckily there seemed to be only one large hallway that stretched on for ages. I could see the light disappearing at the other end, and I hoped that I wasn't about to lose her. I sped up, and reached the end of the hallway, only slightly breathless. It opened into a huge courtyard, lit by huge basins of fire where the flames seemed to be dancing on water.

The nymph was dancing around the basin at the furthest end of the courtyard. She looked beautiful, the flowers and leaves entwined in her hair glinting in the firelight, her strange outfit swishing around her.

She smiled and waved at me, beckoning me over.

Don't go. Be smart, Ruby, the reasonable voice in my head tried to warn me away, but I needed answers more than I needed caution.

As I walked toward her, she giggled, her voice a melody of beautiful notes and tones.

I trained my eyes on the floor, trying to avoid making direct eye contact.

"Who are you?" I asked her bluntly.

"A friend of the queen. Who are you, fair human girl?" she asked sweetly.

"Ruby."

"Like the stone," she replied, laughing.

"I saw you earlier," I replied as sternly as I could. "What were you doing? Were you messing with the minds of the villagers?"

The nymph giggled again.

"You almost caught me today." She sighed. "Crafty humans…the queen won't like that. She doesn't like nosy little people. You're even more curious than the last one."

"What do you mean?" I asked sharply.

"Oops." She laughed again, and before I could get a straight answer out of her she fled. I tried to follow her, running down another corridor that led off the courtyard, but it was in complete darkness and I couldn't see any evidence of her glow.

I walked slowly back to my and Ash's room.

What did the nymph mean?

Had there been other humans who had come here? Was Queen Trina also kidnapping humans as well? We were obviously hugely beneficial to sentries, so it was likely that Queen Trina would have indulged in the same practice as Tejus and his brothers…especially with the Imperial trials coming up. I hadn't really given much thought to what the human-stealing policy was in the rest of Nevertide's kingdoms.

I thought about what the nymph had said. *More curious than the last one.* I felt like it implied that the human she was referring to wasn't around anymore.

Where had their curiosity gotten them?

Julian

Queen Trina hadn't exaggerated the hostility of the dungeons.

I had no idea how long I'd been down here. I could see next to nothing, as no window allowed in light, and whenever the door to my cell was opened to shove in disgusting stew-like food, it was shut abruptly. The walls that kept me in were thick stone, and damp enough to make me think that these dungeons were close to the sea—deep underground. I had a chamber pot, which I kept at the furthest point away from me, and a hole in the middle of the floor that I was to empty my waste into. The smell in the room was even worse than that of Jenus' cellar within Hellswan kingdom. I would have happily traded prisons in a heartbeat if I could.

It also seemed like escape was a complete impossibility.

My only weapon was a spoon that I had stopped using for food. I had spent all the endless hours of spare time sharpening the edges on the stone. It worried me that they'd even left me with any kind of metal object. It indicated that the chance I would get to use it was pretty non-existent.

In the beginning, when I'd first been escorted down here—by two ministers, who had begun brutally syphoning off my energy as soon as they laid their hands on me so that I was woozy and compliant—I had spent hours peering from the small barred hole in the door, hoping that one of the nymphs would get bored and come to make mischief. My plan would have been to bargain with them, for anything, to get me out of here. I guessed that nymphs rarely had true loyalty to anyone other than themselves, and might be willing to go behind Queen Trina's back for the right price. But no one ever came. I saw no signs of glowing light, heard no sound other than the constant dripping from water running through the stones.

The total solitude also meant that I had nothing to do

for hours but think. Or, more accurately, regret.

I wished that I had spoken to Hazel or Ruby about Benedict before being stupid enough to follow him on my own. If I hadn't been so judgmental of the girls' decisions and their help with the trials, then I doubted that I would have ended up in this situation. Before I had believed that Ruby and Hazel were breaking the group apart by spending all their time with the sentries, when all along it had been me and my attitude that had caused a rift in the group. I should have listened to Jenney, been less pig-headed about everything, and maybe we could have all helped Benedict and together removed him from being a pawn in whatever sick game Queen Trina was playing.

I worried about him and Ruby. When I first arrived I had thought that she might be down here as well, the last thing I'd seen before I was taken by the Queen was Ruby's body lying helpless on the ground with Benedict standing above her. Maybe Ruby had been taken back to the Seraq kingdom, but they had kept us separated to add to our misery. I had called out into the blackness of the dungeons a couple of times when I first arrived, but only my own echo had answered me, so after a while I'd stopped. It was too depressing.

I had to accept the idea that my friends had most likely

left Nevertide by now. The idea left me feeling completely alone and more isolated than I'd thought was possible, but I also realized that my chances of getting out of here without GASP investigating would be slim. However, I also had to accept that even if GASP did manage to locate Nevertide, all their focus would be on the Hellswan kingdom. Why would anyone bother to look for me here? I couldn't recall the journey to the dungeons at all, but I didn't doubt that they would be well hidden—judging by the state of them, and the lack of occupancy, they probably hadn't been used in centuries.

After I'd given up looking for the nymphs, I'd made a pact with myself. If I truly couldn't bear to be down here a moment longer—really and truly, like I was going half-crazy—I would ask Queen Trina to reverse my decision. She had originally said that I couldn't change my mind, but if my friends were gone, she might feel more disposed to have me wandering around the castle anyway. Perhaps I could be useful to her in some way? Get a job as a servant or something, and try to avoid the nymphs till I could figure out an escape. I didn't regret my decision to choose the dungeons over free rein in the palace yet. As hellish as this was, it would have been worse to lose my mind completely—to believe that I was enjoying Queen Trina's hospitality, perhaps even refusing to leave when GASP came to rescue me.

But when the time came, when any hope I had was well and truly down the gutter, if Queen Trina disagreed and refused me, then I had my knife. It was my alternate option to spending a lifetime in this cell. Maybe there would be more adventures for me in the afterlife than this one.

ROSE

We arrived in the small village of Murkbeech. Corrine had transported us here: me and Caleb, Claudia and Yuri, and Ashley and Landis. We hadn't spoken at all while we'd waited for Corrine to work her magic, and as soon as we landed in the small village that led to the camp, the silence became deafening as we looked around at the dim sky and gray desolation of the place.

When I'd pictured Murkbeech village, I'd recalled a cozy-looking general store, a quaint gift shop and a grocery shop with fresh vegetables laid out neatly in rows under a bright canopy. Now the shops were empty—windows smashed, no lights coming from within, and rotting vegetables littering the street.

Something had gone horribly wrong here.

"It looks like a ghost town," Claudia murmured as she picked up a carton of milk from the side of the road. "This is dated from two weeks ago, look."

I inspected the label. She was right. Which meant that all this destruction was relatively new. I had half hoped before we arrived that Murkbeech was having a huge problem with their electric and phone signals. It wouldn't have been that surprising given their location, but it was all too obvious that something far more sinister was going on.

I felt sick with worry, and for the first time in a long time, utterly hysterical with fear that I was trying to keep under wraps for everyone else's sake. I also knew that the more we treated this like a routine investigation, like we'd done countless times before, the higher our chances of success would be. The more we panicked, the more foolish decisions we would make, and then...well. It didn't even bear thinking about.

"Let's head toward the camp," I replied to Claudia, gesturing to the others to follow the dirt track that led out of the village and up to the main house. Caleb took my hand and gave a quick squeeze as we moved forward with supernatural speed. Our eyes met briefly, and I could see the same fear I had reflected back in him.

As we approached the camp house, the sign 'Murkbeech Adventures' written above the sprawling one-story building, I felt my heart sink. It was in almost complete darkness apart from a flickering strip light coming from one of the outhouses to the right of the building. Next to the entrance was the camp bus, or what was left of it. It looked like it had been lit on fire, the paintwork black and singed, and the front engine just a shell that exposed the basic framework.

What the hell happened here?

Sticking together, we continued along the track, alert for the slightest sound or indication that there might be someone around.

"It's too quiet," Landis murmured. "But I can sense something…"

His sentence trailed off, but I knew exactly what he meant. I could feel *something*—a tension that was starting to build, and a feeling that we were being watched from the trees that surrounded the camp on either side. I didn't know if it was the place that was giving me the creeps, or something real that was about to jump out at us.

It wasn't long before we found out.

We heard a loud bang, like a door being swung shut. Then from behind the back of the camp, dark, human-shaped silhouettes emerged, running toward us.

"What on earth?" hissed Claudia as we instinctively grouped closer together, readying ourselves for the attack.

As they got closer, I could start to make out their faces—human ones, but mindless, their eyes dead-looking with no sign of intelligent life within their forms. They looked filthy, as if none of them had bathed in weeks, and all of them gaunt to the point of emaciation.

"They're only human," I said. "We've got to try not to hurt them."

I questioned the wisdom of that as one came lumbering toward me—a woman in her mid-forties, trying to slash at my face with mud-caked fingers, her face contorted into a vicious grimace. I knocked her down and she lay motionless on the floor. Before I could check if she was still alive, another one came tearing toward me. I kicked him back, seeing that my husband was doing exactly the same on my right. There were about a hundred of them in total.

"They're like Bloodless," Ashley gasped as she slammed her fist into the face of a teenager. He put up a good fight, more athletic than some of the others, but soon enough his butt was in the dirt.

"They're definitely not Bloodless," Corrine replied, knocking over eight at once with a spell.

"Anyone seen our kids?" Claudia asked as she heaved another body into the pile of groaning humans in front of her.

We all shook our heads. I didn't know if it was a good sign or not…

Soon we had a large pile of bodies in front of us—thankfully all alive, but certainly worse for wear.

"We need to restrain them," Caleb said, heading in the direction of the camp house. "I suggest you all stay here and keep an eye on them. I'm going into the house."

"I'll come with you," I told him, hurrying to his side.

Caleb and I walked up to the camp in silence. I was half afraid of what we might find inside, but also hoping that perhaps our kids were hiding somewhere, away from the crazed humans.

As soon as we stepped inside, Caleb tried flicking the light switch, but nothing happened.

"Power's out," he murmured, checking out a broken lamp on a side table. "I'm surprised they don't have a backup generator here…but maybe with the refurbishment they didn't bother putting one in."

We picked our way through broken furniture and strewn rubbish to the first dorm. None of the beds were made, and the smell in here was particularly pungent. I looked around, using my vampire vision to see if I could see any belongings of the kids, but I didn't see anything I recognized. We checked the other dorms, but everything was in such a mess it was difficult to distinguish individual items.

We were about to leave the last dorm and head back when something caught my eye. It was a black t-shirt with a bright neon logo on it, crumpled up on one of the beds. I made my way over and picked it up. It belonged to my son.

"Caleb, look." I held it up.

He walked toward me, and then lightly touched the fabric of the shirt.

"They left in a hurry, then," he commented, his voice low.

I nodded. "And there," I said, spying a cell phone on the bed. "I think this is Benedict's."

Trying to switch it on, I found it was completely dead—which wasn't surprising, just frustrating. I looked around at the other beds more closely. A lot of them had mobiles lying on pillows. The camp must have asked them to leave them behind during activities.

"We'll charge it up somewhere and see if it helps us." Caleb took the phone, and I gathered the t-shirt in my backpack. I wasn't sure how much help it would be, but I wasn't going to leave it here anyway.

We searched the rest of the house, and, on finding it deserted, we swiftly made our way back to the rest of the group.

"Did you see... anything, in there?" Ashley asked, her face paler than even a vampire's should be.

I swallowed. "No sign of our kids. Just Benedict's cell and some others. Which is why they weren't calling," I replied.

As I gazed over the humans Corrine was keeping in check with her magic, most of them still woozy from our attack, I started to realize that there were three groups emerging: those who were children, and the guests of the camp; the camp organizers, all wearing something to distinguish them, like a 'Murkbeech' t-shirt or badge; and those I presumed came from the village—mostly slightly older, including one woman who looked like she was near eighty.

"What has happened to all of them?" I whispered.

"Let's try to see if any of them will talk," Caleb

commented, surveying the group for those who looked as if they were coming to. He walked over to a teenaged boy. Through the mud and bloodstains that covered him – along with a badly healed stab-wound, I could faintly make out blond hair and blue eyes.

"Hi." Caleb knelt down to his level. "Can you understand me?"

The boy looked at him uncomprehendingly for a few moments, and then his gaze turned to me, standing behind Caleb.

"I recognize you," he whispered. "Do you still want my sunscreen?"

"Wha—Who are you? Do you know your name?" I asked, confused by the question. His accent was definitely British, and he was well-spoken.

"I'm nobody," he sighed, as he started to look around him.

"Do you know where you are?" I asked again.

"Nowhere," he replied and frowned. "Do you want my sunscreen or not?"

"Why does he keep talking about sunscreen?" I asked Caleb in whisper.

"I'm not sure…" Caleb began.

"I wonder if he thinks you're Hazel?" Corrine said. "It

might be why he thinks he recognizes you…and who else but your daughter would need sunscreen in Scotland?"

"I'm Hazel," I said hurriedly to the boy, willing to go along with his delusion to help jog his memory. "Do you remember me?"

"Hazel." He smiled, nodding dreamily.

"Who did this to you?" I asked again. I could hear my own question being echoed by Claudia, who was speaking to another woman at the next tree along.

"It was the dreams," he replied quietly, "the dreams took us…left us empty."

I glanced at Caleb and he shook his head. Corrine was frowning. Clearly none of us had any idea what he could be referring to. *Dreams? What dreams?*

"I had a younger brother, and friends, do you remember them?" I prompted, getting desperate for the boy to make some sense.

He shook his head. "Just the black shadows that came from the sea. Black eyes, black eyes…black eyes…"

He started to repeat himself on a loop, knocking his head into the bark of the tree.

"I'm wondering if you should sedate him, Corrine. I'm worried he's going to hurt himself – and we need to clean up that wound," I muttered.

"I don't know if that's a good idea," she replied, staring down at the young man. "Their minds have already been altered. Perhaps it's best to leave them alone for now until we can help them properly."

"Are you thinking we should take them all back to The Shade?" I asked in surprise. There were a lot of them here to fit in our island's hospital.

"No, just a few. Maybe the most talkative ones, the ones who don't seem so far gone. We will be able to do more than modern medicine can—and then we can take our time questioning them…though I fear it's going to be a long process." Corrine grimaced.

Claudia and Yuri, who'd started trying to talk to the humans, approached us.

"Can't get any sense out of them," Claudia said worriedly. "One woman was muttering about creatures that came from the sea…"

"So was mine… Merfolk again?" I said, even as I knew that was a stupid suggestion. Merfolk shouldn't have this kind of mental effect on people.

"I think we're dealing with something else," Yuri said darkly.

"The jetty should just be down there." I pointed off in the opposite direction to the camp. "We should take a look."

"What about this lot?" asked Ashley, coming to join us.

"We're going to take a few to The Shade, the rest to the nearest hospital. They need medical attention right away—it doesn't look like they've eaten properly for ages."

I shuddered, praying once again that Hazel and Benedict and the rest of the kids wouldn't be in the same state. Wherever they were.

We walked down to the jetty that backed into the sea. There weren't any boats tethered to it, and apart from the lack of people, I couldn't see anything particularly unusual. Caleb joined us as we stood at the water's edge.

"I managed to get through to the local hospital on my phone. An air ambulance will be here soon."

"Did they get any calls from this area before?" I asked.

Caleb shook his head.

"The woman I spoke to on the phone said she had thought it was unusual—normally at least someone at the camp has an accident each year, no matter how minor."

I wished they would have come and checked.

"Come here!" Landis called.

He was standing a few yards off, looking into the mud. As we walked over he bent down to pick something up. It was a long key chain, with a wallet at one end and a belt clip at the other.

"This belongs to Julian," he stated, his face ashen.

Ashley gave a short cry and rushed forward to take the wallet. Her husband held her as she turned her face away from the rest of us.

I approached the spot where Landis was standing. The mud and grassland that surrounded the camp had been filled with the footprints of what I'd assumed was the crazed mob of humans, but here I could make out slightly larger, heavier prints left in the earth.

"Look at this," I called to the group.

"Looks too big to be human," Claudia breathed.

I noticed that there were more of them. We followed the larger footprints, leading down to the jetty where they stopped abruptly.

"Well," I said, "unless whoever these footsteps belong to is able to walk on water, we can guess how they got away."

"You think they've been taken," Claudia said quietly.

I couldn't say the words out loud, so I just nodded.

The pain and fear was indescribable, and all I could do in that moment was stand still, the ground feeling unsteady beneath my feet.

Caleb took my hand again.

"We're going to find them," he said firmly.

I nodded.

At least we had a plan. We'd take a sample of these humans back to Meadow Hospital, where our jinn and witches would attempt to get through to them and discover some answers. As soon as we got even an inkling of what happened here or where our kids might be, we'd summon every single ally GASP had in both the human and supernatural dimensions if that was what it took.

I didn't know what person or creature would be so daring as to target children of The Shade. They must have been living under a rock for the last several years if they didn't know about GASP. But whether they'd known or not, they would soon.

Because nobody messed with the Novaks.

Epilogue: Benjamin

I looked across at my daughter and new son-in-law. We were all sitting in the living room, waiting for River to bring in some refreshments. They had just arrived back from their honeymoon in the Alps, both looking tanned, relaxed and happy. I still couldn't believe how grown-up Grace was now – to her mother and me (especially me), she would always be our baby.

"Who was the better skier?" I asked, smirking at Lawrence.

He rolled his eyes. "Easily Grace – unfair fae advantage."

Grace poked him playfully. "I thought you handled

yourself pretty well…you beat me down the mountain a few times."

Lawrence quirked an eyebrow at my daughter. "I think you let me win."

River came through, carrying a tray of some of Corrine's special herbal tea, and planted it on the coffee table before coming over to sit next to me.

"Was it as beautiful as the brochure?" River asked as I placed my arm around her.

"It was *amazing,*" Grace gushed.

The two of them filled us in with the details of their holiday, and I smiled at my wife's enraptured face. There was nothing that brought her more joy than seeing her family happy.

"Where's Field?" Grace asked. "I wanted to give him a present. I got something for the other Hawk boys too."

River smiled. "Field's hanging out with Maura. As for the rest of…"

She trailed off as the doorbell rang.

"Oh, that could be Field now, actually…" She rose to get the door.

"We need to fully unpack," Grace said. "We brought back so many gifts for you guys. It's just a shame Mom can't enjoy any chocolates, because Lawrence and I spent like an hour in the best chocolatier in all of Switz—"

"Ben," River called from the front door, her voice unnaturally tense.

Obviously it wasn't Field.

I excused myself, and went to join her.

Mona was standing on the landing next to River, and I smiled as I saw her – but then, next to her, I laid eyes on a very familiar face. One I hadn't seen in a long time. One I wasn't entirely sure I ever wanted to see again.

"Sherus," I stated in surprise.

"My apologies for the unexpected arrival," he murmured.

River had gone pale – no doubt remembering the last time we had seen Sherus, and the obstacles he had set me in order to win my freedom from The Underworld. But we both ought to be profoundly grateful to the man. He was the reason that Grace existed - the reason that I was standing here at all.

I cleared my throat. "Sherus. It's been a while… What brings you here?"

The copper-haired fae looked at me, his amber gaze unwavering and deathly solemn. "That I do not quite know, Novak. What I do know is that I need to speak with you and your father… as soon as possible."

READY FOR THE NEXT PART OF THE NOVAK CLAN'S STORY?

Dear Shaddict,

I'm excited to announce that the next book in the series, _ASOV 37: An Empire of Stones_, releases **December 20th, 2016**.

Pre-order your copy now and have it delivered automatically to your reading device on release day.

Visit: www.bellaforrest.net for details.

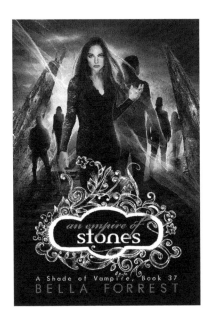

I'll see you in December ☺

Love,

Bella xxx

P.S. Join my VIP email list and I'll send you a personal reminder as soon as I have a new book out. Visit here to sign up: **www.forrestbooks.com**

(You'll also be the first to receive news about movies/TV show as well as other exciting projects that may be coming up!)

P.P.S. Follow The Shade on Instagram and check out some of the beautiful graphics: @ashadeofvampire

You can also come say hi on Facebook:
www.facebook.com/AShadeOfVampire
And Twitter: @ashadeofvampire

Made in the USA
San Bernardino, CA
28 May 2017